An Angel's Tale

A Behind the Scenes Look at Salvation History

FRANCIS ANGELIS

LifeRich Publishing is a registered trademark of The Reader's Digest Association, Inc.

LifeRich Publishing books may be ordered through booksellers or by contacting:

LifeRich Publishing
1663 Liberty Drive
Bloomington, IN 47403
www.liferichpublishing.com
844-686-9607

ISBN: 978-1-4897-3090-9 (sc)
ISBN: 978-1-4897-3091-6 (hc)
ISBN: 978-1-4897-3098-5 (e)

Library of Congress Control Number: 2020917995

Print information available on the last page.

LifeRich Publishing rev. date: 10/13/2020

For Rafael

ACKNOWLEDGEMENTS

I want to thank my wife, Faviola, for her support throughout the process of writing this book. Without her faith and support it would not have been completed. I want to thank Dr. Michael Caplan for his generous financial support but more importantly for his gift of friendship which I value even greater. Finally, I wish to thank all those who offered encouragement through the writing process and whose comments and insight enhanced the final product, especially Fr. Marc Gawronski and Mike Bear.

PREFACE

Sin is the failure to use the freedom that God has given us in a manner consistent with his Will. Throughout this story we see Satan tempt individuals to use their freedom contrary to God's Will. The Lord's Church teaches that temptations come from three distinct sources: the Devil – direct manipulation by the devil or one of the other angels that have followed him; the flesh – disordered desires that are in conflict with the good that God wants for us; and the world – systems and structures that are in place, along with the values that they profess, which are contrary to the Will of God.

For Flesh such distinctions may be important, and who am I to contradict the Lord's Church that lives in the Flesh. But for my part, the sins of the flesh and those of the world are a consequence of that first temptation by Satan in the garden. For this reason (and for literary purposes) this work attributes all temptation to the Devil.

PROLOGUE

Who I am and how I came to be a witness to these (and other) events is a story that goes back to the beginning of time. . . . Before time God was. Time is measured by change – since God, by his nature, is unchanging, when only God existed there was no time.

What follows, because it involves men and women of Flesh, took place in time as a series of events. But because it involves a heavenly plan designed by the Creator, it also took place and continues in the Eternal Now. This mystery of time, related and caught up in the glorious mystery of the incarnation – God made Man – makes it difficult for one such as I, tasked with the responsibility of reporting what has/is happening. As a result, I'm not sure how best to present what I have witnessed. But it seems best to me to start at the beginning and jump to the end. I will fill in the gaps along the way.

I have done my best by striking a balance between the two temporal perspectives. May you see what is meant to be seen and learn what is meant to be learned?

The Story begins near the beginning:

THE REBELLION

*U*pon the throne sat the Glorious One. He that is and has always been. It is impossible to describe him accurately, except by his attributes for he simply IS. He is perfect, and in his perfection he is perfectly good. He is All-Powerful and as a result he is the source of all power. He is all-knowing, yet because that knowledge rests in the Eternal Now, it does not in any way interfere with one's free choices. About the throne was a myriad of angels. Each angel in turn would fly from the throne only to return to give praise and honor and glory. "Holy, holy, holy, is the God and creator." Back and forth they flew. Standing next to the throne was a mighty angel, Michael was his name. And he stood guard. Michael often wondered why he stood guard, because he knew his creator God was all powerful. Why would he need a defender? Michael had once gotten the nerve to ask him.

"If I choose to share my power by asking you to be my defender, what is it to you? Am I not free to do as I wish?"

"Why of course your Majesty! I just meant that given your power, it seems to be a rather useless position. I would rather be giving you praise and honor as the others do."

"You give me praise and honor by doing what I created you for and by no other way. If you did not stand guard, you could not serve me."

"Then stand guard I will your Majesty."

That had been some time ago, as angels measure time, as done on earth it was immeasurable. Yet at times Michael could not help feeling a slight sense of uselessness. At other times, however, he felt a tinge of pride at the thought that his All-Powerful Creator would allow himself, a lowly creature, to share his power. But most times he set aside these thoughts and focused solely on what he had been created to do. He stood guard. He watched as the other angels flew here and there. It was as if they feared to be too close yet, could not bear to be away. Such was the force of his Power and Warmth. To be near him was frightful, but to be away from him was cold and lonely.

Michael also watched the one that sat at the Creator's feet. Each day (if you could call it that) the one sat and listened to the Creator. He was the Most Favored one, and he shared the confidence of the Creator. And then it happened –

Amid all the activity of the angels darting to and fro, his Most Favored one bellowed, "You are going to do what?" It was the first time he had spoken. (It had been his job to listen to the Word.)

"I am going to make Flesh." Said the King calmly.

"But why? Do we not serve you well?"

"Of course you serve me, but as you know, since you have shared in my counsel, I have no need of servants. I chose to share with you and your brethren my divine plan. Likewise, I choose to share with the Flesh that I will create."

"But Flesh will fail you!"

"Ah, is it really my honor you are concerned with?" He paused briefly. "I know that there is a risk that those to whom I offer my Love, through the sharing of what I have, will reject me. That is why I have assigned angels to serve them and to help them reach their goal."

"Which is?"

"Communion with me, of course!"

At the sound of the Most Favored one's voice some (not all, but nearly a third) of the other angels who had been giving praise suddenly stopped. Michael drew his sword and stood ready to protect his Creator. He placed the blade at the Most Favored ones throat, watching for some sign from the Creator to dispatch this insolent one who would dare oppose the Word of the God who had made him. But God simply raised his hand and smiled.

The third that had stopped now circled around the throne, watching what would happen next. This made it difficult, as you might imagine, for the others who continued to offer their praise. Over their joyful, "Holy, holy, holy is the God and Creator!" you could hear him say, "I am going to make Flesh. I'm going to create a place where Flesh can dwell. And I will make there a Holy People. They will know my goodness in a special way and you will serve them."

"I will not serve Flesh!" Sputtered the Most Favored one, as a crowd gathered. The ones who had stopped impeded the flight of the choir that flew to and fro. Still the choir sang out. "Holy, holy, holy, is the God and Creator."

"Not only will you serve them, but one of them will surpass you as the most favored."

"Impossible – that has been my role since forever –"

"Not forever," He interrupted, "but just since I created you."

"Forever I said! You did not create me. I have always existed just as you have." Said the Most Favored, catching out of the corner of his eye the amazed look of those who had stopped.

"Since I created you, you have sat at my feet ready to listen, but today you have stopped listening and have spoken." He continued. "Not only will one replace you as the most favored, but although you sat at my feet, the other will sit beside me." As he said this, he swept his arm and for the first time I noticed another throne beside him. I can't say that it wasn't there always but only that it was then that I first noticed it. In his presence, he commands attention. "And by your actions, you will help select the one who will supplant you. And although only one will supplant you as most favored, I will raise all of those who wish to be my sons and daughters."

"But what about us?" The one who had spoken (for I could no longer call him Most Favored) asked. "Do we not give you praise?" Is not our praise sufficient? Why would you do such a thing? Can you not make us you sons instead?"

Michael could hardly restrain himself as he stood watch.

"That will not be. But you and your brethren may assist them to become my sons and daughters."

"Never!" exclaimed the one who had spoken. "I am spirit like you, I will not serve Flesh!"

"You were made to serve God." Said the Creator, as if this would satisfy the argument. "As you were able to know my counsel, you will be sent to serve them so that they may be holy as I am holy. And in

3

fact, not only will you assist them to become my sons and daughters, one day the entire heavenly host will worship one of them just as you once worshipped me."

"I will not do it." He said, as he left his place at the foot of the throne, standing now in front of the second throne.

Michael stood between him and the Creator. The ones who had stopped now created a half circle in front of the throne so that they could see more clearly. The rest still sang their chorus, "Holy, holy, holy is the God and Creator." It seemed that the louder the one got, the more lovely their voices sounded.

The one, who despite his arrogance had not removed his gaze from the Creator, now noticed the semi-circle around him. "I will not serve Flesh!" He repeated. "We will not give up our rank." Some of those who had stopped nodded in agreement.

Michael raised his sword, and drove it down toward the one who had spoken. But again the Creator God stayed him. "How dare you attempt to destroy that which I created?" He said, sounding like a father scolding his son.

The one who had spoken used this distraction to move away from the throne and took a position in the center of the half-circle created by those who looked on. "I am spirit and will not serve Flesh. As God is spirit I too am god!" He exclaimed as he turned to the third that had stopped. "I offer you a choice which he would not give, will you serve him and the Flesh he creates?"

Not realizing that in stopping they had already ceased to serve him, they said with one voice, "We are spirit and we will not serve Flesh." As they said this they look at each other in amazement. Since the time of their creation they had spoken only the praise of the Creator God.

The one, realizing their amazement, took advantage of the opportunity. "You see all this time he held you prisoner, on an unseen leash, back and forth offering his praise. I set you free. You need not praise him."

Then the Lord, the Creator of all that is, stood. At first he spoke not a word. Yet still some of those who had stopped began to fly back and forth, but the words of praise that they had once spoken would not come forth. Soon, all those who had stopped were flying back and forth.

Simply by looking you could not tell the difference between the ones who had stopped from the ones who continued to sing his praises. But if you listened, you could hear the alternate choruses.

"Holy, holy, holy is the God and Creator!"

"We will not serve! Hooray for the one who freed our tongues."

As the competing choruses reached a crescendo, he let forth all his Glory and those who had stopped began to flee, for there is no room in Heaven for anything that opposes him in his Glory. Michael saw this as a sign and he rose, raising his sword he cast out those who had opposed the Lord. The one who had once been the Most Favored fled at the sword that had just moments before been stayed by the hand of the Lord. He knew now that it would not be stayed a second time. As he fled he bellowed. "We will go to set up our own kingdom where we need not worship and we need not serve Flesh."

"Leave you must, to the place prepared for you. From now on you shall no longer be called Most Favored, but Satan, since you have made yourself an adversary to Me. Now Go!"

THE PLACE OF DESOLATION

· ◆ ◆ ◆ ◆ ·

*W*ith that I found myself, along with Satan and all those who had stopped, in a new place. Understand it is not as if we traveled there, but there we were. Although I knew it was not true, I heard him say: "See I have created a new kingdom." I don't know why the others, the ones who had stopped, did not recognize this as a lie. Then he called out. "Satan ha! I shall choose my own name and it shall be Lucifer. Because I was first and I saw the first light, and only I among all the other angels have known his counsel." The others cheered at his defiance.

The first thing I noticed in this new place was that it was dark and cold. Although the others did not seem to understand, I knew it was because we had left the presence of the Light and Warmth. It was not simply cold, but unbearably cold. Satan alone seemed to notice the cold also. "We must build a fire." He declared. "In Heaven, he disguised the source of his warmth." He lied. "But I will make it open for all to see." With that he struck his staff (I don't know where it had come from) and a spark flew starting a fire about the place. Despite the new fire, it seemed little improvement. Satan (for I refuse to call him by the name he claimed for himself) ordered some of the others to begin stoking the fire with more and more coal. Soon the fires were blazing, yet they did little to improve the lighting or add to the comfort of the place. Instead the fires seemed to be nothing more than a child's play toy next to the real thing, a mockery of the Light and Warmth that is God.

The second thing that I noticed was that the ones who had stopped, (except for the ones whom Satan had commanded to stoke the fires) all seemed to be fluttering around aimlessly. Again what was so obvious to me, they failed to grasp. Before the throne of God, they served as they had been created. Having rejected that purpose, they knew not what to do. As with the cold, Satan seemed to grasp this just as I had. Again he spoke, and again he lied. "He created you to serve him but he made you robots without choice. It was I that gave you the power to say that you would not serve Flesh. In return you must now serve me."

"We will serve you." Replied the others. And as they had in the throne room they began to fly back and forth. This time singing (if you could call it that, it sounded more like a taunt.) "The one who freed us, has become our master." As I watched closer, I noticed that although it appeared to be as in the throne room, upon examination it became clear that it was not the same. Here, their coming and going were motivated by a different factor. In the throne room it was holy awe that cause the angels to leave and fear of being away that caused them to return. Here, it was fear of their new master that made them leave and it was fear of the consequences if they did not, that made them return. I did not understand why the others did not recognize that in the throne room they were not under any compulsion. Their praise was freely given. Here they have exchanged freedom for a chain of fear.

The next thing I noticed was a great chasm. As with the cold and the aimless wandering I seemed to know something that the others were not aware of. There was no reaching the other side. As before, Satan seemed to understand this too. And again he spoke but this time he spoke what I somehow knew to be at least partially true. "Do you see this chasm? It has been made to separate you from him. You cannot reach the other side. Should you attempt you will fall for all eternity."

The truth was that it had been created by their rebellion which separated them from their Creator. I thought, *"The boastful shall not stand before your eyes."*

I can't tell you how long it stayed this way because as I've said before, angels measure time differently than here on earth. But through all that time I can say that I neither stoked the fires nor served the other. I simply watched. To my relief, Satan did not seem to notice. But anyway after some time I noticed (Satan did too) some of the others defecting. They apparently concluded, after having lost eternal joy with the Creator, that it was better to be in a never-ending free fall, so long as they could be away from Satan.

As I watched, I noticed that the angels approached the edge of the abyss differently. Some simply jumped over the precipice in resignation over the hopelessness of their condition. Others, accepting the futility of the effort to reach the other sided, plunged headlong into the chasm as a complete rejection of their erroneous choice. Still others seemed to disbelieve the reality that the other side was unattainable. These leapt toward the other side, straining with all their might to reach the cliff that would reunite them with the Creator. Some of these came close, but nevertheless fell just as those who had merely tumbled over the edge. After a while, I too headed for the cliff, not knowing what compelled me. It was only then that Satan noticed me.

"Stop!" He yelled. The others who were also on their way to escape heeded his command and returned to their appointed tasks. Whether it was fear or respect that made them stop, I do not know. I alone ignored him as I lunged for the other side. Despite my efforts, I barely made it half way. As I dropped below the level of the cliff, I was certain that those who had nearly reached the other side could not have desired to be reunited with their Creator more than I. But in the end it seemed our fate would be the same.

As I fell, I could hear the screams of those who had fallen before me. I heard some cursing the Creator, others were cursing Satan or at least their decision to follow him. But others I could hear exclaiming, "Out of the depths I cry to you Lord, Lord hear my cry. For with the Lord is Kindness in him there is full redemption." As for me I found myself echoing the chorus that had filled the throne room. "Holy, holy, holy is the God and Creator."

I can't tell you how long I fell. With the assorted cries of the others, I must confess it was maddening. But still I continued my refrain. "Holy, holy, holy is the God and Creator." As I looked down to see if I could catch a glimpse of the others it seemed to me that it was getting lighter. I also noticed that I had begun to shake off the cold damp feeling I had experienced since first arriving at the place of darkness. Finally, beyond all expectations it seemed my descent seemed to be slowing. Next, against all hope, it seemed that my ears were deceiving me, because instead of the maddening babble of those below me, I thought I could hear the choir of the throne room joining me in my song of praise. "Holy, holy, holy is the God and Creator." Then, to my surprise and joy, I found myself back in the throne room at the feet of the One who made me.

THE RETURN

As I appeared Michael drew his sword and prepared to strike, but the King stayed his hand and smiled. "Welcome home!" He said.

"Then it was not true that there is no chance to get back?" I asked.

"For those angels who separate themselves from Me there is no return."

"Then how am I back?" I asked cautiously, for fear that he would remedy the apparent mistake.

"You did not stop!"

It was not until he had said this that I realized that he was right. (Of course he was, in him there is no deception.) I mean that I realized that I had not been with those who had stopped. In the Presence you are not aware of yourself, but now as he reminded me it came back to me. I had not stopped. I was darting through those who had stopped when they turned and fled, I was knocked back in the confusion. I tried to get to the King but could not.

"I knew I didn't belong there. Is that why I seemed to know things that they didn't?"

"By their choice they entered into the darkness. In the dark they could not see what they could have seen before. By their choice, they changed their very nature."

"But what of Satan? He knew too."

"He knew because I wanted him to. He still serves my purpose."

"And the others?"

"That you need not know." He said sternly, as a caution against over curiosity. "But now you must go back."

"What?" I exclaimed, sounding too much like the other, I bowed in apology.

"You were sent –"

"Sent?" I interrupted without realizing it. He patiently smiled.

"Do you not yet realize that you were there because I wanted you there? While you were there, I sheltered you beneath my wings. That was why Satan did not notice you. You returned because I called you. Satan noticed you then because I wanted him to. You will be my witness so that others will know. You will return and suggest to him that he needs to have a biographer who will record his every move. Appeal to his pride, it is his weakness."

"Lord I know you know all things, so forgive me for asking, but why will he trust me to get so close once he knows I have returned to you?"

"Tell him I sent you away – It is true. But he will see it differently, his choice has clouded his vision of the truth. He will think that I banished you as a punishment for a traitorous act (for that is what he would have done.) He will believe that you, like him, will harbor resentment for the perceived banishment."

At that moment I realized that I would go back. Either I'd go back freely to do his Will, or I'd go back because that is the place reserved for those who refuse. So I went back with joy to serve the Lord.

Again, as with the first time I can't say I traveled there, but I arrived there just the same. I stood before Satan and to my surprise he seemed to be expecting me. "I knew he wouldn't let you stay." And louder, for the others he said, "See, he has no mercy for us! He has no love for you. He will make his Flesh to be his new slaves. We will make them realize that they too need not serve."

Unlike before the cold did not seem to affect me. I was now aware that, just as he had said, I was sheltered in the warmth of his mantle. Still Satan's lying words rang sour in my ears. Without fear I spoke. "You are right, he sent me back. Tell me, who will know of your great revolt?"

The idea struck him and he smiled. I continued, knowing that the words I spoke came from him who sent me. "You sat at the feet of him who set all things in motion. Now use that knowledge you gained and I will record all that you do and in doing we will show who really has the power!" I was surprised how easily the words came. Clearly the One who had made me had given me a well-trained tongue. I was even more surprised that Satan so easily accepted that the words I spoke about 'who really has the power' were meant to be about him. "When the time is right, you will challenge him and set yourself against all that he has made. Someone should be there to record the triumph!"

Satan ordered all those with him to stop as he stood upon the hard stone that he had fashioned into a chair. As with the fire, it was a poor substitute for the Real Throne. But as if it had been anticipated, there was a spot for me to sit at his feet, as he had sat at the feet of the Lord. He spoke loudly. "This one has been banished by the Lord after his defection from us here. But I will show him more mercy. Rather than banish him for his attempt, I will make him my scribe. He will record our triumph. MY triumph!" And so I sat, uncomfortably close to the one I despised, but all the while knowing that the Lord held me close and would not let me fall into despair.

THE END

As I mentioned, time has no real meaning in Heaven and words such as beginning or end are useful concepts for discussing these things with Flesh. Until such time as the rebellion has ended and Satan, and those who had rebelled with him, have bowed before the Lord the story continues. Likewise, as long as there are people to learn of these things there will not be a true ending. Nevertheless, for each one that we angels have called Flesh, but he calls Beloved, there is an end. What follows are just two examples so that the reader may understand.

The Glorious One sat on his majestic throne. I stood near the throne. Next to me but slightly behind stood Satan. We stood off in a distance. The accuser did not wish to draw too close to the throne. Before the throne stood a man, somehow I knew he had just died. It was then that I understood Satan's reticence to approach the throne. He too feared his everlasting judgment. In an instant the throne transformed from the golden chair of which I was accustomed to a more austere throne which I knew to be the Judgement Seat.

The one before the throne stood there silently. In less than a moment – for time has no meaning here – I saw all that the man had done in his life. All his faults, all his sins were laid bare. All pretense, any façade he had worn was stripped away. He stood there naked before the Judge. No longer was he in the image of the One seated on the throne, but disfigured by the wrongful choices he had made.

Satan smiled as he saw the man's grotesque figure. If he was capable of joy, I would have said he was joyful at the prospect of another soul, like a greedy gambler itching to rake in his winnings. Instead, I would say he looked hungry. His hatred for humankind and his desire to deprive God the joy when one enters into Heaven, was all-consuming.

The man, for his part, stood without emotion. I couldn't tell whether he failed to speak because he was awe struck or defiant. But from somewhere I heard a voice say, "Lord, it is my fault he suffered from concupiscence – have mercy on him."

Another said, "Please Lord – I suffered from the same temptations. They were unbearable! Please have mercy on him."

Then, as if on cue, a chorus of voices came to his defense, either claiming they were responsible in some way for placing him in a bad situation, or for some reason the choice was not fully his. His father spoke and said he should have been there for him. A teacher said she should have been more patient. Still the chorus rang out.

Above all, the accuser shouted – "But he had free choice. He did the deeds!"

The man finally spoke. "Lord I know that I have sinned greatly – but I have been generous with my time, talent, and treasure." As he said this I groaned silently.

"Yeah – put it on the scale. See if he deserves Heaven." Taunted Satan.

"Good one sir." I whispered.

Realizing what he had done, the man continued. "I only meant that I have used what you have given me wisely. I know I can never earn Heaven."

"Look at the scale! Look at the scale!" Bellowed Satan, his voice revealing an insatiable desire.

Even a quick glance at the scale revealed that it was no contest, yet the one on the throne withheld judgment. "There is one more I would like to hear from."

A woman approached the throne. As I said time and age are meaningless here, but her appearance seemed to oscillate between that of a young girl and a woman of uncertain age. She knelt before the throne and bowed. The King stepped from his throne and took her hand. "What would you say my queen?"

"Lord, our Son suffered so much – would his suffering be in vain?" As she said this a tear trickled down her cheek. The King gently took his finger to catch it. "In Heaven there will be no tears but yours my sorrowful queen." He took the tear and placed it on the scale and immediately the scales shifted and the balance swung in the man's favor. "Pray for us at the hour of our death!" The man said. "Now I truly understand the meaning of that phrase."

"I am ready to render judgment!" Declared the King. "His sins warrant punishment and in justice he should be condemned." . . . At this the man's knees buckled under the weight of the judgment. . . . "But in mercy he has been found with sufficient grace."

Turning to the man he said. "You have escaped eternal damnation because of grace. Eternal salvation has been given you, but you are not yet ready to enter into Heaven. Into the purifying fires you must go until such time as your attachment to these sins has been burned away and the temporal consequences of your sins have ended."

And with that the man was gone.

"No!" Screamed Satan – "You saw the man, by justice he belonged to me." His anger at having lost a soul caused him to forget his fear of the Light.

"I thought I heard your voice in the shadows." Said the King.

"You do not play fair." He said.

Michael stepped from beside the throne and approached him. The King raised his hand to stay Michael's advance. "Thank you my prince." Turning to Satan he said: "You have nothing to do with that man. Yet I created him. And I died for him." The voice sounded younger. "And it is by my efforts that he was able to make the few righteous choice he made." He finished in an airy voice. "Am I not able to be generous with my grace?"

"It is grace that you deny us!"

"We have gone over this. You are not Flesh, you are of a different nature." Turning to Michael he said, "Escort our visitors out."

With that word Michael flew towards us and raised his sword. As we fled, Satan complained, "His justice is so thorough, yet his mercy is unfair."

"That is true sir." I said. *Mercy and Justice have met!* I thought.

A second time the majestic throne transformed to the Judgment Seat and before it stood a man. He stood straight, eyes forward, looking directly at the one on the throne. As the one before, he transformed in an instant. As each sin was revealed the man became less and less like the image of his Creator, the man he was created to be. When it was finished what stood before the Lord was a pity to behold.

And again the chorus began.

"Lord, concupiscence is my fault – have mercy."

Still the man stood straight.

From the throne I heard in that younger voice, "I died for him."

The Queen of Heaven appeared before the judgment seat and said, "Please! Our Son's suffering should not be so lightly disregarded."

"I own my choices. I wouldn't have done things differently." Said the man who stood before the throne.

"Have you no fear of the Lord?" Cried an airy voice from the throne.

"That's right," said Satan. "He made this world as it is. Now he would judge you because you navigated it according to his law – survival of the fittest."

"I need not tell you Satan," Began the Glorious One. "But for the benefit of the accused, survival of the fittest is indeed the mechanism by which I allowed the various species to evolve. But man was created as the pinnacle of creation. The evolution intended for humankind was of a spiritual nature."

The man stood there as if in thought. Then he spoke. "Look, I came up in a neighborhood where you either kicked ass or got your ass kicked. I don't regret that – it made me tough. I learned how to keep my head up and take care of myself. I fought to get out and once I got out I fought to get on top." There was anger in his voice as he glared at the King.

From the crowd I heard, "I too suffered in a tough neighborhood. It changes your perception. To admit weakness or vulnerability could mean death. Please have mercy!"

"That no longer matters." Said the King to the voice. Turning to the man, he said, "I am truly sorry for your struggle. The effects of original sin have been a source of so much pain."

"It's my fault!" Cried a woman from somewhere. "I should not have listened. Have mercy on him."

"Original Sin!" Satan scoffed. "Free will! Those are his excuses. An All-Powerful omniscient God could have saved you from all that."

"*He lies!*" I thought. I said, "That is true sir."

"You too had free will." Said the King to Satan. "It was by your own choice that you have put yourself in opposition to me." To the man, he said kindly, "Do you remember your prayers? Say an Our Father for me."

The man began, "Our Father, who art in Heaven …"

"What's his purpose?" Satan asked.

"Who can know the mind of the Lord?" I answered. "*That's it,*" I thought – "*get to the next line. For it is not the Will of the Father that any should be lost.*"

"Thy kingdom come –" the man stopped abruptly. "Your kingdom! Why your kingdom? Your way has brought turmoil on the earth."

"That's right!" Encouraged Satan. "There have been more people killed in the name of religion than in wars."

"*Not true!*" I thought.

"Will you finish the prayer?" Asked the King.

"Please finish the prayer!" Begged the Queen.

"Say the prayer." I silently pleaded.

"Your will is all you have to call your own." Taunted Satan.

"Will you finish the prayer?" Asked the King again.

"NO!" The man shouted. "It was by sheer act of will that I made it out of that neighborhood…"

"Not true," said a voice of an elderly woman.

He paused as if he recognized the voice but continued. "Where were you," he glared at the King, "when I was running for my life? And you –"he said turning to the queen. "Where were you when I had to work two jobs and try to go to college?"

"Please you do not understand. Say the prayer!" Was her reply.

"*Where were you when the earth was formed? Do you know the ordinances of the heavens can you put their plan into effect on earth?*" I thought.

"I did what I did and I'm not sorry. If I bent a few rules or hurt somebody along the way, so be it. No one seemed too worked up about it when it happened to me."

"I did." Said the younger voice from the throne. I watched as the king's features revealed wounds on his hands and feet. The majestic robes became a tattered tunic, shredded by the centurion's whip. The golden crown transformed into one of thorns, no longer comfortably resting on his head but instead the bloody grooves carved by the thorns marred his majestic face.

Still the man remained defiant. The tears of the queen and her entreating could not convince him to change his attitude. On the throne, the beaten and bloodied figure seemed to grimace in pain as if struck again with a cord as he announced the sentence. "By your choice you have rejected the grace offered you and have chosen Hell. Be gone to the place reserved for those who do not choose the Good."

AND SO IT BEGINS

I don't know how long it was, nor how I knew, but some time after the rebellion the home for Flesh was created. So I said to Satan. "It has started."

"So it has." He said. And louder to the others, "He has thrown down the gauntlet. He has made a place for his Flesh to dwell. It is a garden with all the pleasures that Flesh can experience." (How he knew this, I do not know, but I knew it to be true.) How can we see this as anything but a provocation? He held us chained in the throne room to serve him. But this Flesh he has created, he gave them the freedom to roam."

As he said this we found ourselves in the throne room. The contrast between the dark was even starker now that the author of the darkness stood before the true Light. I fought the urge to bow, knowing to do so now would not serve the One who had made me. Instead, I simply lowered my eyes in silent unnoticed homage.

"So you have gone through with your plans to make Flesh." Satan started. "They will disappoint you."

"Look at these two. They have tended my garden and have served me well. Without my request they offer me sacrifice in recognition that I am the source of all they have."

"Of course they follow you. In that garden you have not denied them anything, not so with us. Even though we had served you longer, you denied us sonship and have reserved it for them."

"You, who sat and listened for so long, should know that you were denied nothing that would not cause you harm. And in the same way, they have been denied the knowledge of good and evil."

"They have not been told about the good and the evil?" Satan queried. "What if they should desire evil? You never told us that we had the freedom to choose."

"You were created to know and did not need to be told. Since obviously you chose."

"And them?" Satan asked, clearly fishing, so I was surprised when the Lord replied.

"I placed them in the garden and told the truth. If they taste the knowledge of good and the evil, they will die."

"If they fail, will you make us your sons?"

"A son sees to the work of the Father. In setting yourselves against me you have shown that you cannot be sons."

"And if they fail?" He persisted.

"Some no doubt will. If a third of my angels and the one who was once my Most Favored would rebel, how can I expect them all to succeed?"

"Then why bother?" Satan taunted.

"If these should fail, I'll make more. In the fullness of time, one such as these will serve me perfectly. It is to him the heavenly host will bow before."

"And if not?"

"I AM patient."

"But you must have a plan. If the one you made to be perfect fails, will you accept us as sons?"

"As I said before, one will replace you as the Most Favored and sit at my right hand. Yet if the one to whom the heavenly host is to give its praise should fail to do my will, then I will admit defeat and raise you up."

I must admit, I nearly lost it when I heard him say this. It is not in his nature to boast so he must have been sure. *"But to risk the entire Kingdom on something so fragile as Flesh…"* Before I could finish the thought Satan and I were walking in the Garden. The breeze was rustling the leaves of the trees and I could see the two he had made frolicking in the water. It was obvious that they enjoyed the bodily senses he had given them. The sight of their pleasure made Satan seethe.

"Do you see how he spoils them?" He asked. "He has not only given them bodies to enjoy the pleasures of the flesh, but also a soul that they might live forever." As Satan was speaking, the Lord appeared. He walked with them and they rejoiced in his presence. As they walked through the garden the trees gave up their fruit at the slightest touch. The man and woman, that's what he called them, made no effort, but still offered back to him a portion of their harvest.

"Thanks be to God who provides for all our needs." The one named Adam said.

Shortly afterwards he left them and Satan approached and asked, "Are you not favored?"

"He has provided for all are needs." They said in unison.

"But which of you is most favored?"

"We don't know what that means." They answered in unison

"When you don't walk with him," Satan gestured with his head. "Who walks in front?"

"We walk side by side, because that is how he made us."

"Were you made at the same time?" He asked, frustrated that he had not made them understand the concept of being first.

"Oh no! The other was made first, and I came from him." Said the woman.

"So you are in charge!" He said, as he turned to the man.

"No! You are wrong again! She is bone of my bone, flesh of my flesh, we are equal in his eyes. He is in charge of both of us."

"He is in charge!" Satan taunted, sensing an opening. "Then you are his servants?"

"No, you still do not understand." Said Eve, for that was the name the man would later give her. "All this is his and he has given it over to us to tend. We share his work and he shares his Glory. This last remark seemed to send Satan into a quiet rage which he struggled to control. He gained his composure and bid them farewell.

When we returned to the abyss, he let loose his furry. "Do you see how he mocks us? In Heaven, we could only perceive his Glory but were not permitted to share it. But these, this Flesh –." He sputtered the word.

"They lie!" He screamed, not finishing his earlier thought. "How can I tell who he intends to supplant me with if they won't tell me who is most favored as between themselves?"

"Maybe it's true!" I started. "Maybe they can't tell you who is first because they are one?"

"Impossible!" He bellowed, looking at me sharply.

He did not know that I was not fooled by his earlier lie about not being made. "You were before all others." I offered. "That made you his favorite?"

"Exactly!"

The next day, as is measures on earth, we again entered the garden. The two were playing with the animals. The man called each by its name, and again Satan ranted. "How is it that this Flesh gets to name the works of his hands? We were never given such a privilege." He said with contempt.

"How very unfair." I said, but I thought – "*No, but you were given the chance to help these two become like him. He was willing to entrust the care of these, who he obviously loves, into your hands – and you refused.*"

"Why do they stay so far from the center of the garden I wonder?" He said to no one. "Those trees have fruit that is better than all the rest."

"Hey you!" He called to them. "Did you not see those trees in the center of the garden?"

"Oh yes. They are the Tree of Life and the Tree of the Knowledge of Good and Evil."

A light went on in Satan's face as he recalled the Creator's words. "They have been denied the knowledge of good and evil." He whispered to himself. "That is how I will do it!" He whispered to me. "If they won't tell me who is most favored amongst themselves, I will destroy them both."

"Do you think it will work?" I asked, hoping to conceal my fear that it might.

"The Tree of Knowledge of Good and Evil?" His voice trailing off as if to invite a response. When none came, he continued. "Do you now know good and evil that you don't eat from the tree?"

"Oh No! Here in the Garden all is good. What need would we have of the knowledge of evil? Oh look, here comes the Lord, we will ask him."

At the mention of the Lord's name Satan flinched. "We must return to our place." He said to them. "There will be a more opportune time!" He said to me as we left.

The next day we were in the Garden again. "Did he really tell you not to eat from the trees in the Garden?"

"What kind of a question is that?" Asked the man. "You know we may eat from the trees, for you have seen us eating."

"He has said only that 'you must not eat from the tree that is in the middle of the Garden.' We must not touch it, or we will die." Continued the woman.

"Which tree?"

"Why the one we were speaking of only yesterday. After you left we asked him why we should not eat from it."

"And what did he tell you?"

"We just told you." Said the man, a sort of pitying frustration rising. "He said that we should not eat from it or even touch it or we would die."

"What does to die mean?" Satan asked with a smile on his face. His voice mocked innocence.

"I do not know!" Replied the woman.

"That is because he has forbidden you to know the knowledge of good and evil. How do you know you do not want to die?" He asked.

She paused for a moment as the question had perplexed her. She looked to Adam.

"We should not be talking to this one I fear." He whispered to her. Although I heard him, Satan did not. Adam silently motioned for her to leave.

"That is a good question. How do we know that it is not good to die?" She asked, directing her question to Adam.

"Because he has not given it to us." He answered. "See in this garden we have all that we need. All that is good for us he has given –"

"But what if there is more?" Satan interrupted. "He knows that if you taste of that fruit you will be like him and will know what is good and evil. You will know what to die means and you can choose for yourselves then."

With that she took a piece of fruit.

"Any difference?" Satan asked.

"What is difference?" She asked.

"Difference is change. See there is no difference you have not died. See he lied! He told you that even if you touched it you would die."

"*Not so!*" I thought. "*He only said that if you eat you would die.*"

"He is right!" She said. "There is no change. I have touched it and not died, whatever that means." Turning to Adam, She took a bite. As she took the bite, her eyes first blazed, as she tasted all that is good. But in an instance her expression changed to one of anguish and despair. Next her face showed fear and hatred. Fear of the one who had tempted her, hatred for her companion who had failed to protect her.

"What have you done?" He exclaimed.

"It was pleasing to the eyes and good for food, and I desired the knowledge." She said softly, exhausted as from battle. "I now know I do not want to die. But it is too late."

"See, again he has lied to you." Satan exclaimed. "She has not died. Won't you taste some too?"

"She has not died yet! But I know he cannot lie." Responded Adam.

"Then die she will!" Satan said, changing his tone. "And you will live forever. Do you see all these creatures? They do not suit you. Do you really want to continue without her?

Puzzle overcame the man's face. He looked to the woman.

"It is not good for man to be alone." She said.

I wanted to cry out, "*You won't be alone. He will still walk through the garden. Do not doubt his power to fix this.*" But I said. "Well done sir."

"Please don't leave me to die alone. Won't you take from the tree also?"

I don't know whether it was fear of being alone or misplaced compassion for her that he did it, but in the end he took the fruit and ate it. At that moment we were back in the throne room. "I did it!" Satan triumphantly shouted.

"Yes you did." Said the Lord, not showing the slightest concern. "And I thank you."

"Thank me?" Satan puzzled.

"You have selected the one who will supplant you as most favored."

"How can that be? They both took the fruit. How can you choose either of them?"

"I did not say it would be one of these, in tempting the woman first, you have chosen a woman to supplant you. Your efforts against My Beloved will be constantly thwarted by a woman and one day a woman will in fact supplant you as Most Favored – most blessed. If you continue to resist my will, you will contend with the offspring of the woman you tempted. But beware, one of her offspring will crush you."

"Ha!" Satan laughed. "How can mere Flesh crush me, a Spirit? Don't think that you can scare me off our bet so easily. This woman, the would-be supplanter, she must still serve your purpose. And the one to whom the angels will give their praise must still do your Will. You have said you are patient – I can be patient too."

With that we were back in the place of the dark.

THE DARKNESS GROWS

*t first it seemed that we would indeed have to be patient. But Satan could not leave the two alone. Satan seemed to get pleasure from harming the ones the Lord had made and loved. The two had lost their privilege of the garden and instead of having the trees freely give up their fruit; they had to labor to eat. Satan was flabbergasted that they still made an offering to him despite all these labors. He tried to talk to them but they would not listen. They knew it was he who had led them to ruin so they ignored him, crying out to the Lord when he approached. "Lord, the enemy pursues my soul. Do not let me be put to shame."

But soon the two had offspring, first one and then another. Satan remembered God's threat and he redoubled his effort. Once he saw the boys playing together. Cain, the oldest, was chasing his brother when he tripped and fell. It was not a bad fall but it caused him to bleed. His brother Abel turned and went to help, but Satan got there first.

"Here, let me help you. That must hurt." He said, nodding to the scraped knee. "It's your mom's fault that it hurts."

"I know – They told us. We're not supposed to talk to you."

"Does your little brother always win?" He asked, trying another angle.

"Win?"

"He was in front, you were behind. That means winning."

"No! I was chasing him. When you chase someone, they have to be in front." Said Cain, sounding like I would suppose a big brother sounds.

"So you could not catch him?" Satan asked sounding sympathetic.

"What do you mean?"

"You said you were chasing him. You chase what you cannot catch. Tell me, is HE the favorite?"

"Cain!" His father called. "Did we not tell you that you should avoid that one?"

"Yes – Yes! Do what your father says. If he had been there for your mom, you wouldn't be in the mess you are now."

Adam came and ushered the boy away. Nevertheless, I thought I saw Satan smile.

Just like that we were back in the place called Hell. Satan turned and looked to one of the angels flying to and fro. "You there! Come here." He said. "Go to the Flesh. I want you to follow one of the offspring. The older one, Cain is his name. Every opportunity you have, I want you to remind him how unfair it is that the younger one is the favorite."

After some time we returned to the Flesh and noticed that the Lord God was talking to the one called Cain. We heard him say: "The Devil has his eyes set on you. But you can resist him if you try. But beware, he knows your weakness."

Despite this warning and encouragement the young one sulked away. "It's not fair that I work so hard to grow that grain and I have to give some back to HIM. He doesn't eat. And I know he doesn't need it. It just gets burned up. What a waste of all my efforts."

"That's right!" Taunted Satan. "Your brother just has to watch those sheep, but you have to sweat to make the Earth give up its grain. You're the oldest, why were you not given the choice of professions? Why was your brother given the best job? Is it because he is the favorite?"

Cain said nothing.

"And why do you still give him anything anyway? Surely that is a habit your parents had when they lived in the Garden and he gave them the fruit of the field for free. But now you work the ground, he doesn't make it easy for you. He made those weeds and thistles just to make your job harder. And you're supposed to thank him for that?"

"If you got rid of your brother, you'd be the new favorite. You could take the easier job." The other angel whispered in his ear

"But he is a man, he cannot simply be thrown away."

"No you're right. But if you strike in the head, like he does to the sheep he will die."

"Die?" He said. "My mother has told us about death. It is not part of the good, but part of the evil."

"Yes I know. He has made evil." Satan lied. "Is that your fault? Is it your mother's?"

"Actually, my father says it is his fault for not protecting her."

"And where is that father of yours now? Is he shielding you from the harsh rays of the sun? How about the unfairness that your brother is not only their favorite, but God's favorite too? Who will protect you if you don't stand up for yourself? There is your brother. Call to him to go with you and when you are alone be rid of him and take your place as the favorite."

We didn't stay to see what happened next. Satan feared that God would come to protect the boy. I hoped that Cain would cry out to God as his parents had taught him – but he did not. He struck his brother and killed him. After that things began to really get out of hand. Satan and his angels roamed about the world taunting and tempting the Flesh. As they began to increase so too did the evil on the Earth. Satan would have me recount all of these various victories. And while I was in his service I grew weary of recording them. But here my purpose is different.

THE RESET

- + - + - ◆ + - + - +

The attacks against the Flesh reached such a height that it seemed that every desire of their hearts conceived evil. Satan and I returned to the throne room and Satan boldly stood before the throne.

"I have done it!" Boasted Satan. "I and the ones who joined me have succeeded in utterly destroying your creation . . ."

"You seem to forget that you too are a creature." The Lord interrupted.

"This Flesh," Satan continued. "They have all rejected you. You denied them knowledge of the evil, by my efforts they have been shown the knowledge of evil and they have chosen it."

"That is true." Said the Lord. "And I regret that they have been so easily corrupted. They seem to prefer the darkness."

"So NOW raise us up! As you promised." Satan demanded ignoring the Lord's musings.

"Again you have interrupted me. I regret that they have so easily been corrupted, but do you see the man named Noah? Despite your efforts, he has remained faithful. He has protected his family from the evil that surrounds it. I am going to destroy all that I have created and start over with him and his family."

In the next moment we were on earth and listening to the Lord speak to the man named Noah. He instructed him to build an arc, a huge boat; to gather within it mating pairs of all the animals; and to supply it with provisions for him and his family and for all the animals. He told Noah that in time he would bring a mighty flood upon the land and that it would destroy all that is not safely protected by the arc.

"And what of my neighbors?" Asked Noah.

"That is so kind of you to consider them." Said the Lord, looking in our direction. To Noah, he continued, "No these neighbors of yours are the reason for this destruction. If you bring them with you they will be a stumbling block to you. You must not allow them to join you."

When he finished he left the man and we were once again in Hell.

"How unfair! How are we to destroy this Flesh, if he retains the power to wipe it out and start over?"

"Maybe you were too bold in your opposition to him?" I suggested tentatively.

Satan looked at me with suspicion, but said, "Continue?"

"You allowed your jealousy and hatred for this Flesh to blind you of your purpose. To win the bet and be raised up! You desire only to discover the woman who would supplant you as Most Favored so as to stop her. And to find the one the heavenly host is to worship and destroy him or at least prevent him from doing God's Will."

"You are correct. I am glad he sent you back, but is there a way that we can be sure that He won't start over again."

"Maybe you can make it a condition of the wager?" I suggested.

Satan again looked at me, this time not with suspicion but with curiosity. "Continue!"

"Tell him that we will no longer pursue the destruction of ALL Flesh. Instead we will only attack that which is necessary to interfere with his Plan, if he will agree to give up the right to destroy the world and start again."

Satan liked my suggestion and decided to take it to the Lord. And as he made this decision, we were again before the throne, and the Source of all creation.

"I think it is unfair that you have retained the right to start over." Satan boldly started.

"I have not restricted you from doing anything within your power to bring about your end, why should I be restricted?"

"I have an idea. . ." Satan replied.

"*I had the idea*." I thought.

"Me and my angels. . ."

"They are my angels," The Lord interrupted.

"The angels with me," Satan continued. "Will no longer set out to destroy all of the Flesh you have made, but will instead focus solely on winning the bet. On finding and deterring the Most Favored and finding and destroying the One to whom you say we will give homage."

"That sounds like a fair arrangement, I will forgo some of that which is in my power and you will restrain some of your wickedness and limit the attacks against My Beloved."

"But how will I know that you will keep your word?"

Michael took a step toward Satan, but the Lord looked to him and nodded and to Satan said, "Your brother Michael has shown great restraint because he has been created to protect Me. He now knows that it is not protection of Me directly that is his concern but of protecting the glory and honor that is due Me. By your question you have suggested that I might deceive you, but you know that I cannot deceive (nor be deceived.) But that you may have a reminder to keep your end of the bargain. . ."

And at that moment we were back on earth, and we watched as Noah and his family led the animals off the arc. I do not know how long the flood waters had covered the earth but it was devastated. I recalled the perfection that had been in the Garden and nearly wept.

I heard the Lord who had been speaking to Noah say, "See, I AM now establishing my Covenant with you and all your descendants that never again will all creatures be destroyed by water. I set my bow in the clouds to serve as a sign of this covenant."

These words seemed to satisfy Satan and he beckoned that we could leave. I wondered if he understood that the Lord's covenant had been with Noah.

Back in Hell Satan was triumphant. "He has made a covenant he cannot break." I made no such covenant. I will renew my attacks and he can do nothing."

"But his covenant was that he would not destroy by water, could he not chose another method?" I asked.

"I guess you're right, we must be more subtle, more selective. But as I see it, until we identify who the Most Favored and the one to whom we must give homage, we can attack almost everyone. But I agree we must act with more restraint and according to our purpose.

Right now there is only this family, these eight, and he has identified

Noah as a righteous man. Destroy the father and we destroy the family. We will attack the father!"

So we returned to earth and saw that the Lord had left Noah. Satan looked for ways to ensnare Noah, but he remained faithful to the Lord.

It did not take long for him to devise a plan. Prior to the Flood, Noah was a tiller of the soil and in time he planted a vineyard. When harvest time came he made wine. Satan whispered to him, "You are the first to plant a vineyard. You should celebrate your harvested." We watched Noah taste his vintage and saw that he had drank too much. Satan tried to stir up Noah and suggested he could use his drunkenness as an excuse to carouse around the town. But Noah would not listen and instead went to his tent, undressed, and fell asleep naked.

Satan whispered to his sons. "Did you see your father stagger into his tent? It is a disgrace and to think you must abide by him."

Shem, the oldest responded, "He is our father and we must do his will. He saved us from the flood."

Trying another angle Satan whispered, "But do you not care that he was drunk and there is no one to watch over him." This thought caused Shem to become worried so he sent his brother Ham into the tent to check on his father. We didn't go in the tent and watch what happened but when Ham returned and told his brothers that he had seen their father's nakedness, there was quite an uproar. Satan tried to encourage the other two to do likewise, but they grabbed a cloak and walked backwards to cover Noah's nakedness.

When Noah woke up and discovered what had happened, he cursed Ham for what he had done. Turning to Shem who had made sure that his nakedness was covered, he said, "Blessed be the Lord, the God of Shem!"

"That's it!" Satan exclaimed, not bothering to hear the rest of it. "Did you hear it?"

"I must have missed it," I honestly admitted.

"Noah, has proven himself unworthy by getting drunk. But he blessed Shem saying 'the God of Shem' the one will come through Shem's line."

After that, despite his promise, Satan continued to attack the entire world, although he paid special attention to the line that came from

Shem. It would require volumes to include all that Satan, and the angels that had followed him, did during this time. At one point, Satan had tried to encourage the Flesh to once again strive to be like God, by building their own way to Heaven. The Lord ended that attempt and to slow down the growth of evil he further dispersed them by causing their languages to vary.

THE SIDE BET – AND A HINT
OF WHAT WAS TO COME

＋＋◆◆＋＋

*S*atan continued his attacks on the Lord's Beloved, paying only token heed to his promise to limit his strikes to those necessary to the wager. Occasionally, Satan desired to boast of the devastation he had caused so we would appear before the Lord at the time of our own choosing. At other times, as if summoned, we merely found ourselves before the Throne. One such time Satan asked, "Why have you summoned us?"

"I wish to know what you are about." Said the King.

"I have been wandering across the earth you have created. Look how corrupt this Flesh you created has become." Sneered Satan.

"The Flesh is indeed my creation. The corruption, I regret is your handiwork. But see my servant Job. He is a righteous man, there is none like him upon the earth."

Satan continued. "Of course Job acts righteous. You have protected him on every side. What is this man that you watch over him so? Is he the one?"

The King gave no indication.

"I wager that if you withdraw your protection and allow evil to befall him, he will curse you to your face."

"Satan," started the King. "You know that the soul of even one of them is invaluable to me. What would you put up against something so valuable?"

"I will offer you five souls that I possess."

"Although you have claimed them once they have left my presence at the judgment, they are not actually yours. They have made their choices – but you may not wager them."

"Myself then, I will cease my rebellion for a season."

"For a season?" Asked the King.

"How many souls might you claim if I cease for a season? Would you not risk 99 souls to gain one? I offer you 99 or more, against your one."

"I will accept your wager and will withdraw my protection -- only that you may not strike against his person."

With that we left the throne room and Satan set about to strike out against all that Job had in a single day. First he roused up some Sabeans to strike at his oxen and donkeys, as well as the servants tending them. Next he destroyed his sheepfold and the shepherds watching over them. Next he caused some Chaldeans to attack the men tending his camels. The camels were taken and the men killed. As a final stroke, Satan caused a mighty wind to destroy the home where his children dwelt, killing all of them.

With each tragedy Satan's excitement grew. When Job sons and daughters died, we sought out Job in his home to watch his reaction. The home was simple, made of earth with a thatched roof. A small hearth was in the corner where they prepared their meals. We watched as Job cried out in anguish as he tore his robes. Satan watched anxiously waiting for the curse to come. Instead, Job shaved his head as a form of mourning and said. "Naked I came from my mother's womb, and naked shall I return. The Lord gave and the Lord has taken away. Blessed be the Lord"

With that Satan flew into a rage. Michael appeared to remind him of his wager. So Satan left the place for a season.

It surprised me that Satan was honoring the terms of his wager – until I saw Michael and other angels guarding the Gates of Hell.

"You! Why do you linger?" Satan asked Michael. "Do you not long to return to the warmth of Heaven?"

"You are right, I do miss the warmth and comfort of his presence. But I live to serve and protect his Glory. He is given glory when his Will is done. Here is where he wants me to assure that you will keep your bargain that has brought respite to his Beloved, so here I will stand."

Satan returned to his thoughts as he paced back and forth. "He was so sure of himself when he made that wager. Maybe this Job is the one of whom he spoke."

I too had thought that he might be the one, and wondered what Satan would do next.

"We must stop him!" Satan mumbled. "But how?"

I feared what he would do, so I was shocked when I blurted, "Attack his body."

"That's right – he obsesses over the Flesh. Attack the flesh and the man will fail."

DOUBLE OR NOTHING

nce again we appeared before the King.

"I did not beckon you." Said the Glorious One. "You must know that your desire to return to me is deep seated. You were created to be near me. Did you return to end this rebellion? To kneel before me?" I couldn't help but smile and wonder as I considered the words, "*Every knee must bend...*"

"No!" Spat Satan. "I came to double down on our wager. Your servant Job was spared in his body, allow me to afflict him and he will no longer bless your name."

"What do you propose now?" Asked the King. "He still holds fast his integrity despite all you have done to him. What makes you think you can change that?"

"Flesh!" Satan yelled. "You protected his flesh. Again, let me attack his flesh and if he does not curse you, I will withdraw for two seasons."

"Ok, do as you wish, but you must spare his life."

The wager place, we returned to the home of Job.

An unshaven Job and his wife sat upon the floor in the very clothes that they had torn upon hearing of their children's death. The polished bronze mirror was covered as expected. His wife's eyes were red from crying. Job appeared much older than he had when we last saw him.

Satan looked at him and uttered. "Let your flesh be covered with sores from your head to your toes. Let them ooze with pus and hurt so that it is painful to walk or even breathe."

I watched as sores began to appear. They appeared slowly at first, maybe being nothing more than a pimple but as they grew in number, Job and his wife became worried.

"It is leprosy!" Cried his wife. She covered her mouth and instinctively stepped backwards.

"Impossible!" Exclaimed Job. "I have been in mourning. I have not been in contact with anyone but you and the *minyan*. It must be another trial from the Lord." With that he scooped ashes from the hearth and cast them upon the ground. He sat there and with a broken piece of pottery he scored his face. "Be gracious to me, O Lord, for I am in distress; my eye is wasted away from grief; my soul and my body also."

"He still calls upon the Lord." I said, hiding my excitement. Despite myself, I continued, "Use those close to him to make him realize that such prayers are in vain."

Satan must have concurred with my suggestion because he approached Job's wife and whispered, "It is Job's fault that you have lost everything, including your children. His pride earned him disfavor from God. Let him admit his opposition to God and he will be restored. Let him curse God and I will restore all that he has lost."

I fumed as I heard his lies. Job was not afflicted because of his pride. Satan may be able to restore the man's goods, but only God can restore life. But all of this I could not say.

Satan continued his attack against Job. "He sits there in the dust and ashes thinking his show will hide his guilt. Tell him to admit his unrighteousness and die."

She turned to her husband and said, "Surely you must realize it is only I who sees your show here. Will you insist on your integrity even to me? Go ahead curse your God and welcome death."

Job turned to her and said, "You speak as one of the foolish women would speak." He sounded more condescending than he had intended. So he went to her and held her. "We must accept both the good and the evil from God." And with that he left her in her anger, less she provoke him to sin.

Satan followed him outside deciding to attack him directly. "Does he really treat his friends this way? Maybe you'd be better off as his enemy. Curse him and I will heal your afflictions."

"I shall walk in my integrity; redeem me, and be gracious to me Lord." Was his reply.

As he said this he looked up and saw three of his friends approaching. "We have come to be with you in your time of trouble." One of them said. We didn't stay to watch his companions. Instead, Satan assigned some of those who had followed him to work on the friends. Job's friends listened to their counsel and rather than encourage him, tried to convince him to admit his unrighteousness, but to no avail.

A PEOPLE IS CHOSEN

Since the time of the flood, Satan and his angels tried to turn Flesh from the Lord. It was not an easy task. Once out of frustration Satan vocalized what had been bothering him. "It has been generations since the flood. Not since Noah has he spoke to them! Why do they still look for him?"

"His existence is shown throughout creation." I explained.

Satan eyed me with suspicion, but realized that I had identified the source of the difficulty. "If we cannot keep them from seeking him, we will turn them. We will confuse them, convince them to worship the creation rather than the creator."

And that's what he and his angels did. It was not too difficult really! They are Flesh, and enjoy the wonders of the senses. Satan envied those senses and it was through those sense that he confused them.

We appeared before the throne and Satan bragged. "How will one do your Will when they worship trees and make up their own gods?" The Lord said nothing, so Satan continued. "And with the division you caused by the confusion of their languages, this Flesh you have created has naturally formed into groups along lines of their language. Each group now claims their own god. Who do they worship, since they're not actually worshipping you?" Satan finished with a smirk.

The Lord did not respond, but instead asked. "Do you see my son Abram? He has left all that he has, his family, and his land at my request."

"Is he from the line of Shem?" Satan probed.

"He is!" Answered the Lord. "I AM glad you are paying attention." He said with a smile.

"And what did you have to promise him to obey you?" Satan asked, ignoring the Lord's comment. "You offered us no such promises to gain our compliance."

"As I have mentioned, you are of a different nature. You would not have responded to promises such as those I make with my Beloved. But to answer your question, I promised to make him a great nation and to bless all that bless him and to curse all that curse him."

Upon hearing that, we were gone.

We watched as Abram, took his wife, nephew, and all of his belongings and headed towards Canaan, completing the journey started by his father, Terah. Satan tried to distract him and turn him from his destination but Abram would not be deterred. Abram arrived in Canaan and passed through it while the Canaanites dwelt in the land. We heard the Lord promise Abram that he would give the land to his descendants.

We returned to Hell and Satan wondered aloud. "What is his plan? Certainly he expects more from this man than to complete a journey that his father started."

"Maybe it's the wife?" I said. Wondering why I would help the enemy of the Lord.

"Explain!"

"You remember the Lord said that because you tempted the woman in the Garden, it would be a woman who would become Most Favored? Maybe the One to whom we are to bow comes from her."

"Possibly, but this People consider women little more than property. Surely if one of them were to be the Most Favored, he would have selected one from a society that held women in higher esteem."

"I remind you sir that you and your angels can take the credit for how women are treated. Do you remember in the Garden it was not so."

"What had the woman said?" Satan asked.

"'We walked side by side, because that is how he made us,' as I recall." I answered.

"We will have to see." Was all that he said.

Satan and his angel continued to wreak havoc on the earth. They caused a famine in the land of Canaan, hoping to drive Abram and Sarai from the land. We watched as Abram and his household left Canaan and went to the land of Egypt.

"In Egypt we will disrupt his plan. Look at the woman, she is beautiful. It will be an easy matter to get the Pharaoh to desire her. He will kill Abram and take the woman as his own. There will be no descendant of Shem."

Satan's plan would have worked but just before they entered Egypt, Abram asked his wife to say that she was his sister so that the Egyptians would spare his life. And just as Abram feared the Egyptian officials told Pharaoh of Sarai's beauty and he took her into his house. He rewarded Abram handsomely on her account.

"Abram has been spared." I said. *"And richly blessed because of your interference."* I thought.

"No matter." Said Satan, doubt creeping into his voice. "The man has saved his life by a little deception. The woman will still be taken by Pharaoh and there will be no descendant of Shem. We can deal with him another time." With that he returned to Hell. He did not see Michael, the guardian of the Lord's Glory whispering to the ear of Pharaoh. I followed Satan to Hell and did not know what Michael had whispered until later. We watched as Pharaoh and his household came down with a series of plagues. He summoned Abram and demanded to know why he had lied to him about his wife. He sent them on their way ordering his men to be sure that they left the region.

Some time later we listened as the Lord called Abram in a vision. "Do not fear, Abram! I am your shield I will make your reward great."

But Abram answered him, "Lord, you have blessed me greatly. What more can you give me. I am old and have no heir. Whatever else you give me, it will all go to one of my servants."

But the Lord said to him. "Your own offspring will be your heir. Take a look outside and try to count the stars. As numerous as the stars will be your offspring."

Back in Hell Satan paced back and forth. "How is he going to keep his promise to this one? The man is obviously sterile. And look at his wife, she is old and beyond the age of motherhood. It is beyond reason that this man still follows him. –"

"Sir," I interrupted. "He has sent angels to him, we should go!"

We watched as his messengers left, when it was safe, Satan approached Abram. "What is this he has told you? Surely He is playing you for a fool. You are how old? And still you believe that he can keep his word?"

"He called me many years ago to follow him. I left my family and my land and have followed him. Through all this time he has blessed me in everything that I have undertaken. I cannot doubt him now."

"What of you?" He said, turning to the woman. "I heard you laugh when he made his promise. Your husband has lost all sense, he will die without giving you a son and his servants will inherit his property and you will have nothing. Offer him your servant that she may bear a son that you may claim. This son will be his heir and you will be spared the humility of being childless."

I wanted to scream, "*don't do it, he is capable of doing all that he says and more.*" But I didn't. Instead I said, "Well thought out sir."

Sarai, listened to Satan's suggestion and offered her maidservant Hagar so that Abram could produce an heir through her. In time Hagar became pregnant. Satan used this to try and drive a wedge between Abram and his wife. He whispered to Hagar, "Look, after all these years, your mistress was unable to give her man an heir. You have shown yourself capable of providing the heir he so much desires. Surely, if you approach him, he will choose you over her."

"The child will still be of the line of Shem," I reminded Satan.

"You are correct, but surely it was not what the Lord had planned. Besides, we will put an end to her and her child."

Whether Hagar listened to Satan, or just was acting as a proud mother to be, I don't know, but Satan sought to stir up discord in the household. So Satan whispered to Sarai, "Do you see how she sets herself up so proud? Soon she will claim your husband's love too."

Sarai let Satan's words get to her and she approached Abram. "This is an outrage. I gave you my maidservant so that you might have an heir and since she has become pregnant she forgets her place."

Although Satan tried to bait Abram into reacting harshly, he would not be drawn into it. He simply said, "Your maid is in your power, do with her as you wish."

So Satan returned his efforts on Sarai. "He said you may deal with her as you wish. Treat her so badly that she will want to leave, or maybe lose the baby that she carries. It will not be your fault, you were generous enough to offer her to him. Can he blame you if she could not do the work necessary for her station?" Sarai, again listened to Satan's words and treated Hagar so harshly that she ran away.

Satan's triumph was short lived however. We watched as the Lord approached Hagar by a spring in the wilderness. We could not overhear what he said to her, but eventually she returned to Sarai and bore a son, whom Abram named Ishmael.

"Maybe I was wrong," Satan said.

"About what?" I asked, surprised that he would even consider that he had made an error.

"We could not hear what he said to her," he began. "He is so unfair!" He said distractedly. "We could not hear what he said to her," he continued, "but clearly he induced her to return. He always makes promises to them."

"What then do you propose?" I asked.

"Destroy them of course!" He responded incredulously.

In time, we returned to earth and noticed that the boy had grown, he was now a young man of about 13. The Lord appeared to the man named Abram and this time we could hear what was being said.

"I AM God the Almighty. Walk in my presence and be blameless. I will establish my covenant with you and will multiply you exceedingly."

Satan scoffed as Abram responded to this overture by falling face down before the Lord.

"Here is the covenant which I offer you." The Lord continued. "I will make you the father of a multitude of nations. No longer will you be called Abram but instead Abraham. I will give the land that you are now dwelling in as aliens to you and your descendants. They will be my People and I will be their God."

"What's the price?" Satan whispered to Abram.

"For your part, you and your descendants must keep my covenant throughout the ages. This is the covenant, you and every one of your descendants after you must circumcise the flesh of your foreskin of every male among you. That will be the sign of the covenant."

"Isn't that just like him?" Satan jeered. "He gives them Flesh and then demands that they give it back to him. It's what he did to us! 'Sit at my feet and know my counsel, but don't dare question what it is that I plan.'"

"*Surely you realize that you did not simply question his plan but opposed it.*" I thought. "It is such a small part of the flesh, do you think they will miss it?" I wondered aloud.

"Of course it will make a difference!" Satan said, looking at me with that same incredulous look which caused me to wonder if my true purpose has been revealed. To Abraham he whispered, "It is your male organ. He says he will make you exceedingly fertile yet asks you to slice away your manhood."

Abraham ignored Satan's whisperings and ordered that Ishmael and all the male members of his household be circumcised. Satan tried to stir up opposition among the men of his household, but Abraham was a generous and a good master, and so they complied.

At this same time, God also said, "As for your wife, from now on call her Sarah. I will bless her and she will give rise to nations."

Satan started to whisper to Abraham, "You are old . . ." but before he could complete the thought, Abraham himself fell before the Lord, face down and said "can a man as old as I still have a son? Can a woman as old as Sarah give birth? If only Ishmael could live in your favor!"

I noticed the difference in posture and tone between Abraham's questioning and Satan's original opposition to the announcement that God was going to make Flesh. "*He does not proscribe questions. A thousand questions does not equal a lack of faith.*"

The Glorious One continued. "Your wife Sarah is to give birth to a son and you will call him Isaac. It is with him and his descendants that l will maintain my everlasting covenant. But as for Ishmael, I will honor your request and bless him as well."

With that we returned to Hell. "So now we need not waste further energy attacking the boy Ishmael." Satan started. "But maybe he can be used to further our efforts against the line of Isaac."

In time, God sent his messengers to Abraham and Sarah and renewed his promise of a child. "At the appointed time, around this time next year, I will return and you and your wife will have a son." He said to them.

As the messengers prepared to leave, Abraham offered to accompany them on their way. While they walked, they shared with Abraham that the Lord intended to destroy Sodom and Gomorrah. Upon hearing this, Abraham stopped. Since he had first met the Lord, he had followed him unreservedly. So when he stopped I wondered what would happen. It seemed that the Lord's intended plan was inconsistent with Abraham's understanding of who God is. But through a series of negotiations Abraham was able to get God to agree to forego the destruction of the cities if he could find 10 just men. Although Abraham's efforts were noble, I knew God would not find even ten, Satan had been too thorough.

The Lord carried out his intention to destroy the two cities and their inhabitants, sparing Abraham's kinsman, Lot and his family. Afterwards, just as the Lord had promised, Sarah became pregnant and gave birth to a son whom they named Isaac.

We watched as Isaac grew looking for ways to ensnare him. Satan whispered to him, "See the women around you? See how they look at you when you walk through town. Take one of them to be your wife and settle here. In that way you will secure the promise that your father said God made with him."

But Isaac gave no ear to Satan's whisperings.

After the death of Sarah, Abraham, as if aware of Satan's scheming, became concerned that Isaac would marry a Canaanite. So he sent one of his trusted servants to his kinsman to find a wife for Isaac. The servant met Rebekah, the daughter of his second cousin. Rebekah returned with the servant and married Isaac.

"How is it that Abraham knew of my plan?" Satan fumed when he learned that the servant had returned with Rebekah.

"Who can know?" I replied. *"He trusts the Lord completely. If it was simply a matter of marrying into the Canaanites, he would not need God's promise. He intends to wait for the Lord."* I thought.

After Isaac and Rebekah had been married for some time it became apparent that Rebekah was sterile for they had yet to conceive. Satan whispered to Isaac, "You recall the promise your father spoke of? That his God would make him the father of a multitude through you. Either your father was deceived or you have failed. Either way, you need no longer be faithful to your father's promise."

But Isaac did not listen to Satan and instead entreated the Lord on behalf of his wife that she might become pregnant.

We appeared before throne and Satan spoke. "Why do you bother with this Flesh? Without your constant intervention in the conception process, they would have died out."

"You are mistaken again. Maybe you should have listened longer at the throne." He said kindly. "Yes, I let them participate in the creative act, but I am involved in each and every conception and birth."

"And of this woman?" Satan asked.

"Actually, she will give birth to twins. They will take different paths. One will serve Me, and the other not."

With that information, Satan returned to Hell, while I followed the Lord who spoke to Rebekah. "Two nations are in your womb, two peoples are separating while still within you. But one will be stronger than the other and the older will serve the younger."

When I returned to Hell Satan asked where I had been. "I followed the Lord to see what he would tell the woman."

"And"

"He said much the same as he told you. But he also told her that 'one would be stronger than the other.'"

We watched as Rebekah gave birth to twins as the Lord had spoken. The first to be born was robust obviously stronger than his brother who was born grasping his heel.

"He spoke the truth! The first is obviously the stronger. He is the one that he intends to serve him. But we will fix that."

With that we left, yet we continued to watch as the two grew. The firstborn, they named Esau and he was his father's favorite. It appeared that Satan had been correct. It was obvious that Esau was the one to whom Isaac intended to give the blessings and the promise. The younger, Jacob, was his mother's favorite. She cared for him because he seemed so vulnerable even from his birth. She kept him close to her as he grew.

We watched as Esau grew into a hunter and a wanderer. One day he returned home and saw that Jacob, who never strayed far from home, had just finished cooking a stew. He said to his brother, "I am famished, give me some of what you are cooking."

Satan whispered to Jacob, "He is your rival, will you serve him your whole life?"

So Jacob said to Esau, "First, sell me your right as firstborn."

To Esau, Satan whispered, "What do you care of those things? You have roamed the open country, surely you see there is no need to rely on some promise that you Grandfather's God will give you land in which to dwell. You are strong and need not fear dwelling with the people of the region."

Whether Esau listened to Satan, or was really that hungry, I do not know, but he said to his brother, "I am near death. What good is the right of firstborn if I should die of hunger?"

When we returned to Hell, I asked him, "What good was all that? The promise will still pass to the next generation."

"Yes but it will pass to this weak, mother's boy. He surely cannot be expected to withstand opposition, and he lacks the strength to dispossess the people who dwell there."

Later, as the boys grew and it came time for them to begin thinking of taking a wife, Satan whispered to Esau, "Look around you! See the beautiful women of Canaan. Take for yourself one of these and bind yourself to them and you will be welcomed in their midst and the promise made to your grandfather will be fulfilled." The words of Satan sounded good to Esau so he took wives from among the Hittites.

Finally, there came a time when Isaac was near death. He had lived a long time and his eyes had begun to fail him. He called his son Esau, and as Satan had predicted, Isaac informed Esau that he wished to bestow a blessing on him. "But first," he said "take your bow and arrows and hunt some game for me. Prepare a stew as you know I like, when you have done this I will give you my blessing before I die."

"Isaac does not know that his eldest has given away his right of firstborn. The blessing will go to this one, who has bound himself to these Canaanites but the promise belongs to the younger, weaker one. I could not have planned it better." Satan bragged.

We watched as Esau did as his father directed. Satan returned to Hell confident, that since he had poisoned Esau so that he disregarded his birthright and his kinship relations, the blessing would be for naught. The covenant which the Lord had made with Abraham and

Isaac would fail. He instructed me to remain and watch what happened, so that I could chronicle his success. Esau took his hunting gear and set out for the open country in search of game. While I waited for him to return, I noticed Rebekah call her son Jacob. She had him go and select goats from the flock with which she prepared a stew. She had a conversation with Jacob that I could not hear, but it looked as though he was reluctant to do what she was asking. She took the skin of the goat she had prepared and tied it to his arms. She gave him some of Esau's clothing to wear. She gave him the stew and I heard her say, "Go to your father and say that you are Esau and that you have prepared a stew for him so that he might give you his blessing."

Jacob was obedient to his mother and presented the stew to his father. I watched as Isaac, drew close to the boy so that he might smell him to assure himself that it was Esau. He felt his arms which had been covered by the goat skins. After he had eaten, he blessed him saying:

"The fragrance of my son is like that of a field which the Lord has blessed. May God give to you the dew of the heavens and may the fertility of the earth bring you an abundance of grain and wine. May peoples serve you and bow before you. Be master of your brothers and may the sons of your mother bow to you. Cursed are those who curse you but blessed are those who bless you."

When I relayed all this to Satan he was furious. "That woman has interfered with my plans."

"Remember the Lord's words, 'I will put enmity between you and the woman.'" I reminded him.

Later, when Esau returned to his father and offered him his stew, he was surprised to hear that Isaac had already given out his blessing. "Do you not have a blessing for me also?" He asked. Isaac uttered some words that are not important here, it is enough to say that this "second blessing" did not satisfy Esau and he held a grudge against Jacob afterwards.

Satan tried to fuel this and whispered to him, "Your brother has cheated you out of your right as firstborn and now has stolen your blessing. Be done with him and take back what is yours."

I'm not sure how she knew, but Rebekah was fearful of Esau's anger against Jacob and urged him to go to Laban, her brother. But again,

Jacob questioned her plan. "What will my father think? He is old and dying. How could I leave him now? He will think I am abandoning him, now that he has given me the blessing."

"I will speak to your father. You just prepare yourself to leave, and in the meantime, avoid your brother." So Rebekah spoke with Isaac, and complained how Esau had taken his wives from among the Canaanites. As she expected, Isaac gave permission for her to send Jacob to her brother in search of a wife. Isaac called Jacob and blessed and sent him on his way to Rebekah's brother Laban saying, "May God Almighty bless you and make you fertile, multiply you that you may become an assembly of Peoples."

Back in Hell, Satan was confused. "We must have missed something. This younger one now has both the right to the promise and the blessing."

I was reminded of the remainder of God's word to Rebekah while she was still pregnant. The part I had not conveyed to Satan, "the older will serve the younger."

"So how do we stop this one?" He asked.

"If he has the right to the promise and the blessing, it may not be possible." I said candidly.

"You may be right, but we can surely make things more difficult." And that's what he did. In numerous ways he interfered with Jacob's efforts. Jacob selected Laban's daughter Rachel to be his wife, and Satan convinced Laban to substitute his elder daughter Leah instead. When Joseph discovered the deception he remained steadfast in his determination and offered a second bride price (he had already served Laban seven years as the price of the first) for Rachel. Several times, at Satan's urgings Laban altered Jacob's wages, but each time, Jacob prospered.

Through all this time I wondered if Satan realized that in causing the delay he might be allowing Esau's anger to subside. In the end, Jacob left Laban richly blessed, with two wives, two of his wives' maidservants as concubines, and thirteen children from the four women. And just as I imagined, by the time he met his brother, Esau's anger had abated. For God had richly blessed him as well.

We sat in Hell, Satan, in his mock throne carved in the cold hard stone, and me at his feet. Satan murmured, obviously distressed with the success of the People of Israel, (at some point the Lord changed Jacob's name to Israel). Satan had caused a famine throughout the region – yet the People prospered. They had survived the famine because of the Israel's son Joseph.

"I knew he would be trouble! All that talk of rising above his brothers. He and his dreams! I caused him to be sold into slavery. That should have been the end of it. I miscalculated, I should have followed to make sure he was taken to some backwater."

I thought to myself, "*The enemy dug a pit and fell into it himself.*"

Satan continued, "When I learned that he had been sold to a person of renown I went and caused that he would be thrown into jail. Who would have guessed that the Pharaoh's cupbearer and baker would be thrown in with him? Then they had those dreams which Joseph had been able to interpret. After the baker was released, I did my best to keep him busy, lest he remember his promise to Joseph. But the Pharaoh was a man of dreams too. The baker recalled his promise and brought Joseph to Pharaoh and he interpreted his dreams as well. Even after Joseph had been raised to such a high position I still had a chance. I worked on him when his brothers came to buy grain during the famine, but he would not listen. He remembered his own dream and – How did he put it?"

"'Do not be disturbed because you sold me. For God sent me before you to preserve your life.'" I replied.

"How could he have been so resistant to my attack? How could he have been so confident?"

"*Resist the devil solid in your faith!*" I thought.

Satan finally said, "It is no matter now! I will renew my efforts."

THE COMING OF A SAVIOR –
A SECOND HINT

‡ ‡ ♦ ‡ ‡

*T*he People of God dwelt in Goshen, the land that the Pharaoh had set aside for them and they became prosperous and strong. It bothered me, since they seemed to forget that they had a land of their own promised to them by God.

That the Israelites prospered in Goshen bothered Satan too, but for a different reason. And after some time (like I said time has no meaning here.) Satan complained, "Joseph is gone yet they thrive in the land of Goshen under the protection of Pharaoh."

"But this Pharaoh does not remember Joseph. Maybe they can be driven out of Egypt." I said. *"After all, they have grown comfortable here. The Promised Land is in Canaan."*

Instantly we were in the throne room of Pharaoh. Satan whispered to Pharaoh. "Look at the People who dwell in Goshen. They are outsiders. If war should breakout, they would join the enemies."

"But they have been there since before I became Pharaoh. It is written that one of their kin saved Egypt during a famine and that they were given the land in which to dwell in gratitude."

"That is the gratitude of one of your predecessors. Surely, they have done nothing for you. And look at what they consume. Should another famine occur they will be Egypt's downfall, rather than savior."

Pharaoh listened to the words of Satan and set taskmasters over the People of Israel. He set them burdensome tasks yet still they thrived.

Now Pharaoh did not need Satan's whispering. He had come to fear the resilience of the People of Israel. "Let a force be assembled and wipe out this People." Satan was ecstatic. He could not have expected such a result.

But one of Pharaoh's counselors spoke up, "Then who will build your store cities?"

Satan saw the look on Pharaoh's face. The Counselor's words had struck a chord. Fearing that he would lose his advantage, Satan whispered, "The boys – kill the baby boys. The men who live now can continue to build but without offspring the race will surely die off."

Pharaoh listened to Satan and ordered the Hebrew midwives to kill the male children at birth. But they did not do as Pharaoh commanded so the People of Israel continued to thrive.

Satan whispered to Pharaoh, "These People care nothing for your commands. Make it lawful for your own people to kill the babies. Then you will see this People die off." Pharaoh listened to Satan and he ordered his people to cast the male babies of the Hebrews into the Nile. And they did as he ordered.

Satan and I returned to Heaven. I basked in the Warmth being in the presence of the Lord. I relished these excursions that Satan used to taunt the King, or to press what he considered an advantage. "You have failed!" He boasted.

"What do you mean?" Asked the King.

"This People you have chosen, that you sheltered in Egypt during the famine. It is in Egypt where they will cease to exist."

"Satan," He started, sounding like a father explaining something to a young child. "My Will is not so easily thwarted."

"That is not so!" Satan contradicted. "It was your will that I should sit at your feet and listen, I thwarted your Will when I revolted."

"That is only partly correct. You were created to serve the Lord. And until your revolt, you served me by sitting at my feet and listening. I gave you free will, your revolt only changes how you serve me."

I thought, "*The Lord has made everything for a purpose, even the wicked, for the evil day.*"

The King continued. "It may be delayed, but I assure you every knee will bow and proclaim me Lord."

"Never!" Shouted Satan. "I stopped serving you when I rebelled. I will never again bow before you."

"Have you forgotten our wager? One day you will even bow before this Flesh, which you so despise. At that moment, you will bow before me."

"What nonsense is that?" Satan questioned.

"You came here for a reason?" Asked the King, ignoring Satan's question.

"I came to tell you that your People will be wiped from the face of the earth."

"You are certain that the one of whom I spoke will come from this People?" Asked the King in a light-hearted tone.

Satan hesitated just a moment, reflecting a small doubt. "It must be so. You made your promise to Abraham. You have favored him and his offspring. I even know you have appointed Michael, whom you have set as your own guardian, over this People as well."

"You have learned much, but you still do not understand."

"Michael?" I whispered. "You have said nothing of that before. What make you say that?"

"Silence! Did you not see him whispering in the ear of Pharaoh's counselor?" Satan whispered.

I pondered what it meant that the one created to guard the Glory of the Lord also guarded this People.

We returned to Hell. The stark difference from the Presence of the Lord was almost unbearable, but the Lord sustained me.

Satan paced back and forth considering what the Lord had said. "You have learned much but you still do not understand." He muttered, more to himself. "What is it that I do not understand?"

At that moment we were transported to earth. We watched as Pharaoh's daughter was presented with a basket which her servant had pulled from the reeds. "A baby!" She exclaimed. "A Hebrew baby!"

"You know your father's commands." Satan quickly whispered. "Throw it into the water."

But she took pity on the child and arranged with a Hebrew woman to nurse the child.

Satan beckoned us to leave. "He has defeated us again."

"*You – not us!*" I thought.

So Satan watched the child, whose name was Moses, grow. He looked for ways that he might interfere with God's plan for him.

Satan's first idea was to encourage Pharaoh's daughter to raise him in court to make him as Egyptian as possible. But try as he did, Moses was treated differently. Moses too, even as a young man, sensed that he was different. As he grew he learned the truth that he was a Hebrew and desired to see the People from whom he came. He rode to the store city in his court apparel. We watched as he took in the condition of his People.

Satan whispered, "See what you have been spared? You are not like them."

But as Satan said this, Moses noticed one of the taskmasters beating a man struggling with his burden. "Move! Old man." Said the taskmaster, as he brandished his whip.

"But I normally align the bricks, I don't carry the load, it is too heavy! There are not enough young men to carry anymore." Begged the man.

Moses was enraged at the treatment and approached the taskmaster and struck him. The man lost his balance and fell to his death.

Satan had not expected it but he tried to take advantage of the circumstance. He whispered, "Now you've done it. You must flee. Leave this People, leave this land. They will blame one of the Hebrews. Save yourself."

Instead, Moses looked to see if there were any witnesses. Seeing none, he buried the man in the sand.

Moses returned the next day. I don't know how I knew, but I was aware that he was drawn by the misery he had witnessed and the words that Satan had whispered. 'You have been spared!' "Why?" he asked himself.

As he pondered these things, he noticed two Hebrews fighting each other.

"Stop! What are you doing? Why do you fight each other? Is it not bad enough that the Egyptians strike you?"

One of the men looked up and said, "Who made you a prince and judge over us?"

The words appeared to stun Moses. Again I heard his thoughts.

"Why was I spared, who appointed you prince/judge?" He said, "Why do you say that? Do you know who I am?"

"Yeah, you're a Hebrew that . . ."

Satan recognized his opportunity and quickly whispered, "You have an Egyptian master. Do you need another? He has been here just two days. What happened yesterday when they found the taskmaster? He was long gone – It was you and your People that suffered. He has brought misery with him."

The man listened to Satan and said, "Do you mean to kill me as you did the Egyptian?"

"But how do you know? There was no one around."

"When they found the dead Egyptian they brought all of us that had been working in the area. They demanded to know who did it. They beat us until an old man stepped forward. He said he had suffered under the man but that an Egyptian had rescued him. They said they would look into the Egyptian, but took the old man's admission that he had been beaten by the dead man as evidence of his own guilt. They killed him."

Moses became fearful when he heard that his attack on the Egyptian had become known. Satan whispered to him, "Now you have done it. Your mother cannot help you now. You may dress like an Egyptian but you are a Hebrew who killed an Egyptian."

Moses, fearful of the consequences, left Gosen and fled Egypt. He eventually came to rest in the land of Midian where he took a wife from the daughters of Jethro, a priest. He became a shepherd, tending the flock of his father-in-law.

As we returned to Hell, Satan gloated. "So much for the savior of this People. He attempted to save only one of them and all his efforts got him was a death sentence. He has run away, abandoning them rather than face his punishment. From a position in the court of Pharaoh, he has emptied himself, becoming little more than a slave."

Although Satan was confident that he had successfully dealt with the threat that the man named Moses presented, I continued to watch him. Once when he was tending his father-in-law's sheep he came upon a bush of thorns, aflame but not consumed. Whether he could perceive it or not I do not know, but it was clear to me that it was Michael which caused the flames. As I knew this would be an important moment I sent word to Satan.

"Moses?" Satan exclaimed, "I thought I had rid myself of him." He finished before he noticed the flaming bush. Since Satan was afraid to get too close to Michael, we stood a ways off, watching as Moses turned aside to approach the bush.

From the bush we heard God call out, "Moses, Moses!"

"Here I am." Answered Moses.

"Do not come near! Remove your sandals for you are on holy ground."

"Who are you?" Asked Moses timidly.

"I AM the God of your fathers Abraham, Isaac, and Jacob."

Moses fearing to look at the Lord, hid his face. I noticed Satan also cringing in the Lord's presence and recalled how he and the other angels had fled Heaven so long ago when the Lord showed forth all his Glory.

The Lord explained that he had seen the affliction of the Israelites and had heard their cries. He told Moses that he was going to rescue them from their slavery in Egypt and lead them into a land "flowing with milk and honey," whatever that meant. He ended simply by saying, "Now go! I am sending you to Pharaoh to bring my People, the Israelites out of Egypt."

Satan, still hidden yet fearful that he would lose his bet, whispered to Moses. "Who are you, a mere shepherd? Why would Pharaoh listen to you? Do you not remember that you have killed an Egyptian? Your adopted grandfather the Pharaoh, who may have spared you has died. His son will not be so merciful."

Moses, hearing the whisperings of Satan asked God, "Who am I that I should go to Pharaoh and bring them out of Egypt?"

God answered him, "I will be with you and this will be your sign, when you have brought the People out of Egypt, you will serve God at this mountain."

At the time, it puzzled me that the sign that Moses had been sent would occur after he had accomplished what he had been sent for. But now I consider that it has something to do with the fact that God is in the Eternal Now. Cause and effect – before and after have little meaning in the spiritual realm. In any event, after some further hesitation and doubt raised by Satan, it was agreed that Moses would go and that his brother Aaron would speak for him.

So Moses returned to Egypt and as the Lord had promised, all those who sought to kill him were dead. He presented himself before the elders of the Israelites and with Aaron's help he told them, "The Lord, I AM, the God of your ancestors, the God of Abraham, the God of Isaac, and the God of Jacob, has sent me to you. He has seen you and what you have been suffering and he has decided to lead you out of your slavery and into the land that he promised Abraham. A land flowing with milk and honey."

The elders and the People of Israel came to believe all that Moses had told them. Moses and Aaron went to Pharaoh and said to him, "Thus says the Lord, the God of Israel: 'let my People go, that they may hold a feast for me in the wilderness.'"

But Satan whispered to him, "Who is this God of the Israelites? Is not Pharaoh among the gods of Egypt? You do not know him!"

Pharaoh listened to Satan and replied, "Who is the Lord that I should obey him and let Israel go? I do not know the Lord, and I will not let Israel go."

Moses and Aaron said in reply, "The God of the Hebrews has come to meet us. Let us go a three days journey into the wilderness, that we may offer sacrifice to the Lord, our God, so he does not strike us with the plague or the sword."

"Where did the threat of plague and sword come from?" I wondered, but said nothing.

But Satan whispered, "Who will do the work when they are gone?"

Pharaoh, prompted by Satan's whisperings said, "Why do you make the People neglect their work? Look how numerous they are, and you would have me give them rest from their labors? Off with you!"

Satan smiled as Moses left, dejected. He whispered to him, "Whoever this God of yours is, he has no power here in Egypt. He said he would free this People, and yet they are still here."

"Good one sir." I said, but thought, *"The Lord said that he would allow Pharaoh's heart to be hardened. Do not lose hope."*

To Pharaoh Satan whispered, "This man Moses returns and tries to give the People hope. Increase their burden so that they will no longer listen to him."

And that's what he did. Pharaoh ordered the taskmaster to stop providing the straw, an essential material for brick making, to the Israelites, but to insist that the daily production quota remain the same. Satan's plan had the intended effect. When the news that they would no longer be provided with straw to make the bricks they complained to Pharaoh. He responded, "You are lazy, that is why you ask to go and offer sacrifice to the Lord."

When the Israelite foreman returned from their meeting with Pharaoh that confronted Moses and Aaron. They complained, "You have made us offensive to Pharaoh and his servants, putting a sword into their hands to kill us."

Satan whispered to Moses, "See this People do not want you. Remember what that man asked you so long ago? 'Who appointed you prince and judge?' Return to your wife and family. The sheep you tend are easier to handle than this People."

Moses, despite his insecurity, did not listen to Satan and had recourse to the Lord. As he called out to the Lord, Satan fled, instructing me to remain and watch. I thought, *"Resist the Devil and he will flee!"*

In response to Moses' cry, the Lord spoke. "Now you will see what I will do to Pharaoh. He will not just let the People go, but he will insist. He and his people will drive them out lavishing gifts on them as encouragement.

"I appeared to Abraham, Isaac, and Jacob, but I did not make Myself known to them by My name. Yet I made my covenant with them, promising to give them the land of Canaan. Now I have heard the Israelites' groaning because they have been reduced to slavery by the Egyptians. Therefore, tell the Israelites that the Lord their God will free them from their burdens."

Moses again appeared before Pharaoh and, as the Lord instructed. Moses threw down the staff that the Lord had given him and it turned into a serpent. Pharaoh was amazed, but Satan whispered to the magicians in Pharaoh's court. "That is nothing, do the same and see my power. You need not fear this man." They did as Satan had whispered and to their surprise their staffs turned into snakes as well. Satan turned to me and smiled triumphantly. But I nodded in the direction of the snakes withering on the ground, Satan turned just in time to watch the serpent from Moses' staff devour the last of those conjured by the magicians.

Satan was taken aback, but only for a moment. "What of it?" He whispered to Pharaoh. "Your magicians conjured serpents just as Moses did. You need not heed his request."

In the end Pharaoh refused Moses' request to allow the Israelites to go and worship the Lord. But his face reflected a certain doubt. After this the Lord sent a series of plagues on the Egyptians. The first one occurred when Moses met Pharaoh as he was beginning his day at the Nile. Moses said, "I was sent to give you a message from the Lord. He says, 'Let my People go to serve me in the wilderness. But since you have not yet listened, this is how you will know that I AM the Lord.'" After saying this, Moses lifted the staff in his hand and said, "With this staff I will strike the water in the Nile and it will turn to blood. The fish will die and the water will stink, you and your people will be unable to drink." Aaron took the staff and struck the water and it turned blood red, just as Moses had said.

Satan again whispered to the magicians and they too were able to cause the water to turn red. Emboldened by this feat of his sorcerers Pharaoh refused Moses request.

The Lord delivered on his promise to free his People. It took ever increasing plagues the last one, the death of the Egyptian's first born before Pharaoh relented. We watched as the angel of death descended over the land of Egypt. As it went forth we heard the wailing of mothers in its wake as it took the lives of the first born males throughout the land. When it got to the region of Goshen it turned aside. (Later, I learned that the Lord had instructed Moses to have the People slaughter a lamb and apply its blood to their doorposts as a sign so that the angel of death would pass over that house. The instructions were rather specific and it is a ritual they keep even to this day.)

Despite the obvious loss, Satan insisted on returning to Egypt. Pharaoh had called for Moses and Aaron and instructed the People to leave Egypt at once. Remembering the Lord's promise that the Egyptians would lavish gifts upon them when they left, the Israelites asked the Egyptian people for gold, silver and other items. They were in such a hurry to have the People leave that they willingly gave the Israelites what they asked for. We watched as the People started their journey out of Goshen. It was a site to behold, for the Lord had called down a cloud of smoke to lead them on their journey.

Leaving the region of Goshen we returned to Pharaoh as he sat on his throne surrounded by his counselors who were trying to console him over the loss of his son. Satan approached him and whispered, "This People whom you have let go are the reason your son is dead." He started. "And who will now build your supply cities and do all the work that the Israelites used to do? And what will the surrounding people say when they learn you have let them go without a fight? They will think you weak and take the opportunity of your mourning to attack. You must go after them and make them return, or slaughter them if they refuse!" He finished with a grin.

Pharaoh listened to Satan and ordered his chariots ready and sent them to pursue the Israelites.

Satisfied that he had set things in motion to bring about the destruction of the People, Satan decided to return to the Israelites, still basking in the excitement of their freedom. The first thing we noticed was although there had been no fight in the departure from Egypt, they were arrayed as if for battle. The second thing was that they were not leaving by the most direct path. "What is this?" Satan queried. Seeing the cloud which was set before the People leading them on, Satan whispered to the People. "Has this God of yours no sense of direction?" The People listened to Satan's words as they noticed that the wilderness seemed to be closing up on them. "He has led you into a gauntlet. Even now Pharaoh has readied his chariots and is pursuing you. There will be no escape!"

We retuned instantly to Pharaoh and Satan whispered, "This People whom you have released from bondage is wandering aimlessly in the wilderness. Hurry so you may avenge the death of your son and all the sons of Egypt." Heeding the voice Pharaoh spurred his army forward, sending up a cloud of dust that could be seen for miles.

We returned to the People and it was obvious from the commotion in camp that they had in fact seen the cloud of dust raised by their pursuers. Upon seeing the cloud, some cried out to the Lord. Others began to murmured, first amongst themselves then aloud to Moses, "Were there no burial places in Egypt that you brought us to die in the desert? Why have you rescued us from Egypt? Did we not tell you to leave us alone so that we could continue to serve the Egyptians? It would be better to serve the Egyptians than to die in the wilderness."

But Moses was firm in his resolve and answered them, "Do not fear! Stand your ground and see the victory the Lord will win for you today! For these Egyptian you see pursuing you today, you will never see again. The Lord will fight for you; you have only to keep still."

With that Moses ordered the People to set out toward the Red Sea. (Later I learned that the Lord had spoken to him.) The cloud that had been leading them now moved behind them. Whether it was intended to obscure the Egyptians' view of the Israelites, or to take the Israelites' attention from the dust raised by their pursuers, I do not know. But the action emboldened them so that they took heed of Moses' instructions. As they approached the shoreline, Moses stretched out his arm and raised the staff that the Lord had given him. To the surprise of the Israelites (and Satan's chagrin) the water parted creating for them a path through which to cross.

Satan refused to accept that his plan to finally destroy the People would fail. He relentlessly taunted the Egyptians, "You will let a band of slaves on foot, with livestock and women and children, escape the mighty Egyptian chariots." He sneered. "You must overtake them."

Blinded by the cloud that the Lord had placed between them and the Israelites, and stirred into a foam by Satan's taunts, the Egyptians pursued the People, following them onto the bed of the Red Sea, seemingly heedless of the peril caused by the walls of water on each side. As we watched the chariots began to bog down in the mud of the sea bed. It soon became clear that the People would make it safely to the other shore. As the last of them reached the safety of dry land Moses turned and lowered his arms and the wall of water began to close upon the Egyptians.

Satan, once again defeated by the Lord flew into a rage and ordered that we return to Hell. I lingered just long enough to hear Moses begin,

"I will sing to the Lord, for He is gloriously triumphant; horse and chariot he has cast into the sea."

We did not follow the People closely as they left the Red Sea. Satan sent some of his angels to look for ways to cause discouragement and urge them to long for a return to Egypt. Several times, whether a result of the fallen ones' urgings or simply the natural consequence of a long journey and fear for the needs of their fleshly bodies I do not know, but they murmured against the Lord. They complained about not having enough water, and being hungry. Each time Moses cried out to the Lord and he sent them relief. It was only when they had reached Mount Sinai that Satan seemed to take a more direct interest in them.

We sat amidst the fires of Hell as I listened to Satan blaspheme against the Lord. Suddenly he exclaimed, "It is time to go!" And we were instantly with the People. They were at the base of a mountain wreathed in smoke. Lightning flashed and we could hear peals of thunder. We watched as the People closed their ears. I don't know how I knew, but I was aware the Lord was speaking from the cloud. Apparently Satan was aware too because he whispered to the People, "You have chosen to follow a powerful and fearful God. Return to Egypt and serve their gods. He is giving you a list of commands that you must obey. You saw what he did to the Egyptians when they did not please him."

I must admit, the Lord in all his Glory is a great and terrible display. Remembering how Satan and the angels that followed him fled so long ago when the Lord showed forth his Glory, I was not surprised that the People showed awe for him, but Satan's words turned that awe into fear for many of those present. As a result, the People asked Moses to be their mediator between themselves and the Lord. At the time I thought they had squandered a chance to have an intimate relationship with him.

In any event, the Lord gave the People, through Moses a number of instructions they were to follow. Satan tried to convince the People they were external burdens imposed upon them by an arbitrary and capricious God. (He continues that effort today!) But I realized that they were simply guideposts for right living. They were meant to help the People manage their relations with God and with each other. The People seemed to grasp that because they accepted them and willingly entered into the covenant with the Lord as a sign of their acceptance. But all this is secondary to my purpose.

The real drama occurred after the Lord had given the People these instructions, and Moses had returned up the Mountain. The Lord had promised to set the instructions on stone, presumably to emphasize their permanence. We did not follow Moses up the mountain. It was then that I realized that Satan's whisperings revealed his heart. *"How could someone who had been given the privilege of sitting at the Lord's feet have gotten things so wrong?"* I thought at the time.

I later learned that while Moses was up the mountain God was instructing him on preparations for him to take to fulfill what the Lord had earlier expressed; to make the entire People a "Kingdom of Priests." As I mentioned, Satan was too fearful to approach the mountain to see what was happening between the Lord and Moses. But in his cunningness he recognized his opportunity.

"Now is our chance, he has called away the shepherd. It is time to scatter the flock." To the People he whispered, "Where is this man Moses who has brought you from the safety of Egypt to this wilderness. The last time he ascended the mountain he returned quickly. Are you sure he is returning? Can you trust such a powerful God? Where will you go? You cannot return to Egypt, for he has routed them and you would not be welcomed there. And you know not where Moses was leading you."

Satan's words rang true with the doubt and anxiety many were feeling, so they pondered what they should do. And Satan was ready with an answer. "Make for yourselves a new god. Aaron was Moses' mouthpiece. Go to him and ask that he make for you a god to lead you further."

And that's what they did. "Come, make for us a god who will go before us; as for the man Moses who brought us out of the land of Egypt, we do not know what has happened to him."

To Aaron Satan whispered, "How was it to serve your little brother?" *"He is using the same trick he used on Cain and Esau."* I thought.

To Aaron, Satan continued. "They have been given jewelry and other trinkets of gold from the Egyptians. Do as they wish and you will be the spokesman for god rather than your little brother." He finished with a sneer.

And that's what he did. He ordered the People to hand over the jewelry they had been given and he melted it down and fashioned for them a golden calf. When it was finished, he present it to the People and they exclaimed, "These are your gods, Israel, who brought you up from the land of Egypt."

I have to admit, I missed it but Satan did not. He whispered to Aaron, "Did you hear that? They said 'These gods.' They have recognized you as their god!"

Aaron, buoyed by their exclamation and goaded on by Satan, build an altar and when he had finished, he exclaimed, "Tomorrow is a feast to the lord!" And the next day the People sacrificed burnt offerings. They ate and drank and reveled before the golden calf.

In the midst of their revelry Moses returned. He was carry two tablets inscribed by the Lord with the instructions that had been given. When Moses realized what was happening he cast down the tablets in anger and asked Aaron, "What did this People do to you that you should lead them into a grave sin?"

"Who is this man that you need answer to him?" Satan whispered.

Aaron, ignoring Satan, answered, "Do not let my lord be angry."

"Lord?" Satan taunted. "He is your little brother."

"You know how the People are prone to evil."

"That's it! Blame them – it's not your fault."

"They said to me 'Make us a god to go before us. We do not know what has happened to Moses who brought us out of Egypt.'"

"So I told them to take off any gold they were wearing and cast it into the fire, and this calf came out."

Now as Moses and Aaron were distracted with their conversation, Satan and the other fallen angels took the opportunity to rouse the People into a mad frenzy. What followed was horrible to behold (I later learned of the sadness it caused the Lord.) When Moses and Aaron could not regain control over the People, Moses called on all those who were for the Lord to rally to him. The men from the house of Levi rallied to him and at his instructions slew those who were caught up in the frenzy.

After things settled down, Moses returned up the mountain to beg the Lord to forgive the grave sin of the People. This the Lord did, but as a result of the incident, the Lord indicated that he would no longer go with the Israelites because if he did he would destroy them. What followed were a set of instructions regarding the ritual sacrifices, the construction of a tent, where the Lord might be encountered, and a whole list of rules and regulations. (I will not detail them here, for they are available elsewhere.) To one such as I not made of Flesh they all seemed rather mundane. But I later learned that they were intended to teach the People three things – The Lord is maker of all and cannot be molded into an image of the People's choosing; Sin causes separation from the Lord; and the call to be holy requires one to be set apart from others (even in their midst) to not do as those around you do. I don't know if Flesh gets it yet.

The People ultimately left the mountain and proceeded towards the land promised to their ancestors. On their way Satan and the angels who followed him stirred up discontent, leading the People to complain against Moses, and doubt the Lord. This distrust culminated in an event which added forty years onto their journey and prevented many of those who had left Egypt and had seen his mighty deeds from entering into the land promised to Abraham.

It happened after Moses had sent twelve scouts, one from each of the tribes, to reconnoiter the land into which they were to enter. Upon their return they spoke of the abundance of the land, just as the Lord had promised. But they also spoke of the power and strength of the people of the land.

Satan whispered to the People, "You cannot hope to take the land. You have lost favor with the Lord."

Two of those scouts, Caleb, from the house of Judah and Joshua, from the tribe of Ephraim, stood against the others and declared that they could take the land just as the Lord had promised. Despite their urgings, the People listened to the whisperings of Satan and heeded the word of the other scouts They refused to enter into the land.

Satan and I returned to the throne room. Michael stood ready like a servant eying the hand of his master, ready to dispatch us. But the Lord had welcome in his eyes as he spoke, "What brings you here?"

"Do you see this People that you have wagered your Glory on? You show them your power and might and yet they are turned aside by my mere whisper."

"You are right!" Said the Lord.

"Does that mean you will raise us up?" Satan asked hopefully.

In answer, the Lord spoke to Moses saying: "How long will this People spurn me? How long will they not trust me, despite all the signs I have performed among them? I will strike them with pestilence and disown them. Then I will make of you a nation greater and mightier than they."

I smiled when I heard him but to my surprise Satan remained defiant. "You have said that the one of whom you spoke would come from this People. If you do that then I must win."

As Satan finished we heard from Moses. "The Egyptians will hear of this as will all the surrounding peoples. They will say that you were not able to bring the People into the land. Pardon then, the iniquity of this People in keeping with you great kindness, even as you have forgiven them from Egypt until now."

The Lord is unchanging, so I can't really say he relented, but upon hearing Moses' prayer the Lord said to us, "You see my servant, Moses, how he shepherds this People. I will honor his request."

To Moses, I heard him say, "How long will this wicked community grumble against me? I have heard their grumblings. I will do to them as they have said. Here in the wilderness their dead bodies shall fall and not a single man over the age of twenty shall enter into the Promised Land except Caleb and Joshua. Forty years they shall wander in the wilderness, which corresponds to the forty days that were spent reconnoitering the land."

When he had finished he nodded to Michael who ushered us from the throne room.

When we returned to Hell, I expected Satan to fly into a rage, but instead he sat upon his makeshift throne and rubbed his hands. "You saw his anger! If it wasn't for the pleading of this man Moses, he would have been done with them."

"But he said if he destroyed the People, he would build a new nation from Moses."

"I am more certain that this Moses is the one the Lord has wagered on."

And with that we were again in the midst of the People. We listened as Moses recounted all that the Lord had told him.

Satan whispered to the People, "See you have angered your God. Do you really think he will not go with you as Moses has threatened? He has forgiven your grumblings so many times. Go now and possess the land which he promised your ancestors. He had brought you this far, he will not allow you to fail."

"*You shall not put the Lord to the test.*" I thought. To Satan I said, "You sound like that boy Joshua."

"That was my plan. They do you not realize that it is folly to seek even what the Lord intends for them, in a manner and at a time not according to his Will. They will be destroyed"

The People listened to Satan's whisperings and set out to enter into the land. Despite Moses' warnings that the Lord would not go with them, they entered into the hill country but were driven back in defeat by the Amalekites and Canaanites.

Satan, intent on bringing down Moses, stirred up two separate revolts against him. One of them was political in nature, challenging his primacy by refusing to follow his directions to turn aside from the Promised Land. The other, more religious in nature, challenged Moses and Aaron's position as leaders of the assembly. "The whole community is holy!" They had said. In both cases the Lord affirmed Moses' and Aaron's position and destroyed those who had opposed them.

In any event, the People turned their backs against the Promised Land and began their forty year purgation in the wilderness. During this time they continued their grumblings against the Lord, once it brought them an invasion of deadly snakes. Another involved additional complaints about the availability of water and in the process disclosed that Moses was not the one on whom the Lord had wagered. It is not necessary to recount all of the events of their sojourn in detail, since it is available elsewhere. But what follows seems most significant for my purposes.

Following the destruction of those who challenged Moses' authority, we stood amidst the fires of Hell. The warmth and light they provided were as nothing compared to the True Light. Satan paced back and forth. "Why has he taken such an interest in this People? He was so coy when we last asked. What was it that he said?"

"'You have learned much, but you still do not understand.'" I replied.

Despite Satan's efforts the People continued on their journey to Canaan, the land promised to Abraham. Satan used all his resources to rouse the nations through which the Israelites must pass against them. First there was Edom, their own kinsmen. Moses had sent messengers ahead asking permission to pass through the land. But Satan had whispered into the King's ear. "This is the People who stole your birthright and blessing."

Satan had not been the only one whispering then, for I saw Michael also whisper, "Your ancestor Esau forgave that long ago, for the Lord has richly blessed you as a people."

Whether Satan saw it too I do not know, but Satan continued, "Look, they are like locust. The will devour everything in their path."

Seemingly in response Moses spoke up. "We will not enter any field or vineyard, nor drink from your wells. The Lord has provided us food and drink for the journey."

"You have heard what happened to the Egyptian that followed them into the sea! Their God fights for them." Whispered Satan, again changing his tack. "He has promised to drive out the nations before them. If they enter your land you cannot prevail."

"You have heard of the promise he made to your ancestor Abraham. It was the nations of Canaan that the Lord had promised to clear out. Not yours." Michael answered.

"And what of the Egyptians? What if they pursue them for revenge? If you aid them you must contend against them." Satan countered

In the end, Edom refused to allow Moses and the People of Israel to pass through. It has been a source of contention to this day.

Another time it had involved the nations of Moab and Midian. The People of Israel had camped out in the plains of Moab and Satan went to Balak, the king of Moab, and whispered to him. "Look at that mass of People. They will devour all that they encounter." Balak heeded the words of Satan and went to the king of Midian and warned him of the Israelites.

Now at that time there was a man named Balaam that could discern the Will of God and Balak and the king of Midian went to him with a fee in their hand and said; "There is a People who have come out of Egypt so strong it is as if they cover the earth. They have camped out against me and I fear they will overtake me. I know that those whom you bless are blessed, and those you curse are cursed, so curse this People since they are too mighty for me."

Balaam asked the men to stay the night so that he could consult the Lord as was his custom. But the Lord said to him, "You shall not go with the men. You shall not curse this People for they are blessed." In the morning Balaam told the princes that the Lord had refused to allow him to go with them.

"Why would he give this Flesh so much power?" Satan asked. "Whoever he blesses, the Lord blesses; whoever he curses is cursed."

"It is because he consults the Lord and does as he wills." I answered.

"Maybe he is the one?" Satan pondered. "I can destroy this People and spoil the Lord's prediction at the same time if I can get him to return to Balak." With that we returned to Moab as the princes relayed Balaam's message to the king.

"Who is this that would refuse your request?" Satan whispered to the king. "You must have him curse this People! Appeal to his vanity – send more noble princes to him."

So Balak sent more princes with greater honor and he gave them this message: "Let there be nothing that will prevent you from returning to Balak. He has promised you a great honor and will do whatever you ask."

Satan whispered to Balaam. "You have the power," he said to him. "Do you not hear what people say about you? Whoever you curse is cursed; whoever you bless is blessed." He continued, placing excessive emphasis on "you."

"*The Lord has spoken – He has blessed this People since Abraham.*" I thought. I said, "Maybe he has changed his mind."

Satan and I returned to Heaven and watched as Balaam entreated the Lord. Satan smiled as he heard Balaam's request. To the Lord Satan said, "Do you fear the power of this seer? You claim to trust this Flesh and have given them free will. Why not let Balaam decide whether to bless them or not."

"Surely you do not believe that his blessing is anything without MY blessing?" The Lord responded.

"For some reason you have humbled yourself and allowed this Flesh to share your power. It was you that has allowed him to make a name for himself. If the Moabites believe in him, let him go with them."

So the Lord said to Balaam, "If the men have come to call you, rise go with them; but only do what I tell you."

In the end, Balaam left with the men. Despite his acquiescence to Balaam's desire to go with the men, the Lord was angry that Balaam had chosen to go with them. At the time I thought it a contradiction, but as the events unfolded, I realized that the Truth cannot contradict himself.

Balaam set out riding a donkey, accompanied by two of his servants. The Lord set an angel over the path through which Balaam and the men had to travel. The angel, whom Balaam could not see, was armed with a sword and block the passage. The donkey alone saw him and turned aside into a field. Balaam beat the donkey to make him return to the path. Once again the donkey saw the angel, this time in a narrow passage, and drew back. As she cowered from the angel, she pressed Balaam's leg against the wall. Once again Balaam beat the donkey forcing her to move forward. A third time they set out and again the angel of the Lord went before them, this time taking a position in a passage so narrow that there was no room to turned aside either the right of the left. The donkey, unable to pass or evade the angel, merely laid down and refused to move.

At this point the Lord opened the mouth of the donkey and it began to speak. I don't know whether the donkey actually spoke or the Lord spoke through it, but it said, "Why do you beat me?"

Balaam, not seeming surprised to hear the donkey speak responded, "Because three times you have acted willfully and refused to go, if I had a sword, I'd probably kill you."

"Since you have been riding me have I ever refused to carry you?"

"No?" As he spoke, the Lord opened Balaam's eyes and he saw the angel of the Lord armed with the sword.

The angel lowered his sword and asked, "Why have you beaten your donkey these three times? If it had not turned aside you would have been slain. I have been sent because your decision to go with these men is against God's Will."

"But the Lord told me I could go with them!" Balaam responded indignantly.

"The Lord permitted it because he knew it was the desire of your heart to go and he has given you free will. But he sent me here to dissuade you."

"With each temptation the Lord will provide a way out!" I thought.

"I have sinned!" Replied Balaam. "I will return home."

"No, now you must go with the Men – but speak only what the Lord tells you."

So Balaam continued on his journey and when he arrived he had Balak build seven altars and offer a bull and ram on each. There Balaam spoke the words that the Lord had given him. To Balak's horror Balaam did not curse the Israelites, but in a series of oracles blessed them. Once again Satan's efforts turned against him. Balaam and Balak parted ways and the Israelites passed through unharmed.

THE PROMISED LAND 1.0

he Israelites continued their journey toward the land promised to Abraham, Satan and I watched as they approached the Jordan River. "Surely this young man Joshua is not Moses. How does he propose to cross during the harvest, see the water has overflowed the banks?"

I thought. "*But surely the power rests with God and not the one he chooses to use.*" But said, "You are right sir!"

We watched as the bearer of the Arc of the Covenant waded into the flood plains. Instantly the water from the north stopped and the water piled up like a wall. The water to the south continued flowing, leaving the ground dry for the People to cross. When the last of the People had crossed, the Arc came up on dry land and Joshua built a memorial of twelve stones. The people who lived east of the Jordan feared the People of Israel because they saw that the Lord had stopped the flow of the Jordan so that they could pass through its midst.

It so happened that the crossing of the Jordan coincided with the feast of Passover, which had been established when Moses brought the People out of Egypt. After the Passover the People held a feast from the fruit of the land. On that day, the manna which had fed them though their journey ceased. They were no longer journeying. They were home!

"Look at them!" Satan mocked. "They think they have arrived. Do they think that the people of the region will easily give up their home land? Look the town of Jericho is protected by a strong wall."

Then we saw that as the People approached Jericho, Michael was standing before them with his sword drawn. Joshua approached him and asked, "Are you for us or against us?"

Michael, who must have looked like a man to Joshua said, "No but I am a commander of the Amy of the Lord. Do as I say, and you and the others," he looked in our direction, "will know that the battle for the land is the Lord's"

We watched as Joshua commanded his army to march around the city. We watched as they repeated this march for six days. On the seventh circuit the priests blew their trumpets as Joshua had commanded. We watched as the walls fell.

After this Satan no longer sought to directly intervene in the battle for the land of Canaan. Instead he and the angels that had followed him contended with Michael and the Angels of the Lord. That battle continues to this day. In all this, he continued to seek to discover the identity of the one about whom the Lord spoke.

Satan and I were back in Hell after roaming the earth. "He has all but admitted that the one of which he spoke must come from this race. What is different about this People?"

"They have no king but the Lord," I replied, surprising even myself. "Recall that in the days of Moses the Lord had him appoint 70 men to assist him. After that they appointed judges amongst themselves but they had no king."

"OK, that's true, but what of it?"

"I don't know sir. If you remember, I was meant to watch – you asked what is different and that is what I noticed. If it means anything, I do not know."

"I believe you may have something. Humans are weak. If we can pervert for them their notion of what a king is, maybe they will be unwilling to acknowledge God as King."

"A brilliant plan." I lied. "But will it prevent the coming of the one of whom the Lord spoke?" I truly didn't know the answer to that question but I knew that no good could come of any decision to reject the Lord as their King.

"Look at what the kings of the earth do. A king will take their sons and call them out to war. He will press others to plow his fields, reap his harvest and craft for him instruments of war. For kings of the earth are always about expanding their kingdom. Nor will he spare their daughters. He will take them to be his bakers and cooks. He will levy taxes on their crops and their flocks. How could they continue to call God their king after several generations of such treatment? NO – let these things pervert their understanding of what a king should be and in time they will reject the Lord as King as well. Once they have rejected him as their King, there is no way that the one whom the Lord hopes to supplant me will do his Will."

"But how will we do it?" I asked. "They have followed the tradition of Judges since the days of Moses when the People accepted the Lord as their King in Jeshurun."

"We must look for ways to destroy their reliance on the judges placed before them." Satan answered. And from that moment on Satan looked for ways to attack the men and women appointed as judges. He commanded his followers to keep him apprised of any opportunity they could exploit.

As the years past many judges were appointed. Some were more faithful to the Lord than others. But the pattern seemed to be the same. A Judge would allow, or worse cause, the People to go astray. In such times the Lord would withdraw his protection and they would find themselves oppressed by a neighboring people. Then a new judge would arrive and the People would return to the Lord and they would be redeemed.

We returned to earth and watched Samuel. We watched as he passed on the obligation to judge the People of Israel to his sons, Joel and Abijah. And Satan sent his evil spirits to whisper in their ears and they turned away from the path of their father and took bribes and abused their position. The People of Israel came to Samuel and inquired who would serve as judge since his sons had perverted justice. And Satan stirred up the People of Israel to demand a king as the other nations.

At one point, whether as a result of Satan's constant promptings, or simply because they were dissatisfied at being different from the surrounding nations, the People began to complain. "We have grown tired of the judges that have been placed in our midst. Look at the nations around us, they have a king that unites the people. The king will judge us and united under one king we shall be unbeatable."

"Have you forgotten your history?" I wanted to scream. *"Do you not*

remember when you fought against Amalek and Moses prayed and the Lord went with you. And your enemy was mowed down?" But I said nothing, I was meant to watch. So we watched as Samuel prayed to God.

Satan and I left and returned to the throne room. "Do you not see how the People you have chosen have now rejected you as their King? Are you afraid to allow them to choose their king?"

"You know I have given them (and you) free will. They may do as they will. In fact, I have already told Samuel that he may give the People a king as they desire. But only to warn them of the burdens that the king will bring them."

"You speak of burdens." Satan scoffed. "You have placed burden upon burden on this People of yours."

"What do you mean? My burden is light! The instructions I have given them were for their good to help them stay on target. To help them understand what it meant to be holy."

"Like not planting two different grains in the same field, or combining meat and dairy?" Satan scoffed.

"Do you really think I am concerned with agricultural practices and food combinations? No – those are intended to teach them something about ME. I will not banter with you over these passages. You, who sat at my feet, already know what I sought to teach them, and yet you set yourself against ME. And what about you?" The Lord continued. "What burden have I placed on you?"

"You have denied us flesh. The ability to touch and feel."

"And how has that been a burden to you?" The King asked patiently.

Satan stood there for a moment pondering a reply. But turned to leave without answering.

"I have not dismissed you yet?" The King said sternly. "Answer the question. How has that burdened you?"

"It is not so much a burden," Satan began. "But we were your first and you give that gift to Flesh instead of us."

"I have told you before, you are of a different nature. You are equipped for the tasks which I have shared with you. They have been placed in charge of the physical world, for that they need flesh. You and your kindred were placed in charge of the spiritual world. The flesh that you crave would have been a burden to your work. At some level you understand that because you were made to understand. But you, and those that have followed you, act against your very nature and that is the source of your rebellion. I again urge you to cease this rebellion and bow before me."

Satan was obviously touched, more by the loving tone than the words themselves. But he shook his head and said, "We rejected you as Lord because of your decision to create this Flesh. You have lost your Kingship over this Flesh you have created so now you wish to reestablish it over us? It will not happen!"

As we returned to earth I thought, *"Every knee must bend!"* We returned in time to watch as Samuel anointed Saul as king over Israel. He was a young man, taller than most and handsome to behold.

I won't recount all of the events during Saul's reign where he chose to follow the whisperings of Satan rather than the counsel of the Lord as provided by Samuel. But through Satan's whisperings Saul began to believe that his success as king lay in his own ability and the continued favor of the People. One event, makes the point clearly. Once when the People were being harassed by the Amalekites the Lord sent word to Saul through the prophet Samuel.

"The Lord has instructed you to take revenge against Amalek for his refusal to allow the Israelites to pass through his land as our People fled the Egyptians." Samuel began. "But as you defeat him, put EVERYTHING to the ban. Do not spare him!"

Saul raised his army and advanced against the Amalekites. He was successful in the battle but when it came time to place the spoils under the ban Satan whispered to him. "Surely the Lord did not intend for your men to fight without reward. Will they so readily join you next time if you fail to reward them now? Samuel may have anointed, you but you serve as king only so long as the People are happy with you!" Satan taunted. Saul was visibly shaken by Satan's comments. Satan pressed his advantage. "And what of the Lord? Clearly you would not have been successful if the Lord had not been on your side. Take the best of the flocks and herd and sacrifice them to the Lord."

"Surely the Lord desires obedience more than sacrifice." I thought but said nothing.

Samuel learned that Saul had not followed the instructions

concerning the ban and became angry and went to him. Saul greeted him saying, "The Lord bless you! I have kept the command of the Lord." It was almost as if he was anticipating the reason for Samuel's visit.

"Then why do I hear goats and oxen?" Asked Samuel.

"You are king, you need not answer him." Whispered Satan.

But Samuel held his gaze and Saul stammered, falling back on Satan's earlier arguments. "I kept some for my men and to bring back to sacrifice to the Lord."

Samuel was not persuaded and, echoing my earlier thought, exclaimed, "Does the Lord delight in burnt offerings and sacrifices as much as obedience? The Lord has rejected you as king."

Once again we were present before the Lord and Satan spoke. "I see why you would not let your People have a king."

"As I told you before, I did not prevent them from choosing a king. In fact, my servant Samuel anointed Saul and I sent my spirit upon him. He is obviously not the one of whom I spoke. He has shown that he was not worthy for the task to lead my People, but behold my servant Samuel has found another."

Instantly we were transported to the town of Bethlehem. We watched as a man named Jessie paraded seven of his sons before Samuel. As Flesh goes they all seemed to be excellent specimens, but Samuel was looking for something more, because he was not satisfied with any of them. We were about to leave when Samuel asked, "Are these all your sons?"

"There is another, the youngest, he is tending the sheep." Replied Jessie.

"Send for him, we cannot continue without him."

So Jessie sent for the youth, and when he was brought in, I noticed that like the others, he was ruddy and handsome to behold. But it was his eyes that separated him from his brothers. They were captivating and revealed a sensitive spirit. Samuel watched too as the young man entered. As if on cue he took his horn of oil and anointed him in front of his brothers. I was reminded of Joseph who was singled out among his brothers. Upon seeing the boy Satan turned to leave and we were present before the throne.

"That is to be your king – a mere boy! He has neither strength nor wisdom. What does a shepherd know about leading a people?"

"Moses was a shepherd!" I thought.

"Watch!" Was all the Lord said in response.

Back in Hell Satan wondered aloud whether David was the one of whom the Lord spoke. "But Saul is still king. How will David ascend to the throne? Maybe the boy is a mere trick devised to distract us?"

"He can neither deceive nor be deceived!" I thought. I said, "Perhaps."

Because he was convinced that David had been set up to deflect his attack on Saul, Satan continued to assault Saul. "Who are you that you should be king?" He whispered to Saul. "This is a stiff-necked People. Look at the trouble they gave Moses." He continued, enjoying the torment he was causing.

"Call out to the Lord!" I thought. *"He would not have called you if he had not equipped you."*

But the natural anxiety of ruling a People and Satan's torments continued to work on him. Finally, one of his servants suggested that he find a man of sensitive nature, skillful in playing the lyre. "When you are tormented, let the man play for you and drive the tormenting spirit away." He explained. Saul found the suggestion reasonable and commanded that such a man be found. To my surprise and Satan's delight, the boy David was the one they found to sooth Saul's troubled spirit.

We returned to Hell and Satan asked out loud, "Can we use this to our advantage? Maybe we can destroy Saul and David with one blow!"

Satan continued to watch as David found favor with Saul. We watched as David came out against a Philistine named Goliath with nothing but a sling and a stone. It galled Satan to hear David's boast that it was the Lord that would deliver Goliath into his hands, but we watched nonetheless. "If David fails, as it appears he will, we need not worry about the boy who would be king." Satan mumbled. But David prevailed and cut off Goliath's head with the Philistine's own sword.

We watched as Saul's own son, Johnathan made a covenant with David, pledging loyalty to him. We watched as David continued his campaign against the Philistines, and his fame grew. "That is how this boy will supplant the king and ascend to the throne – by ingratiating himself to the People. It looks like I miscalculated the Lord's plan. He does aim to have this boy take the throne. We must stop it from happening!"

Once when the men were returning from battle the women came out and sang in celebration. Satan turned to me when he heard them sing, "Saul has struck down his thousands, David his ten thousands."

"That is how we will rid ourselves of this boy. We will get Saul to destroy him, while he still reigns." Said Satan. To Saul, he whispered, "Do you not see how they credit David with more than they credit you? He aspires to be king." Saul, listened to Satan and looked for ways to be rid of David.

Satan intensified his tormenting of Saul. As a result, David was called to play the lyre as had been suggested earlier by his attendants. As David played Saul fiddled with his spear. "That youth is who they wish to have king instead of you. Take that spear and pin him to the wall." Whispered Satan.

Saul listened to Satan and cast the spear in David's direction. Yet David evaded the spear twice.

Satan continued his assault on Saul. "Even your God has left you. Send David into battle, he is a youth and not a soldier. Let the Philistines rid him for you." Saul listened to Satan and made David commander of troops despite his youth. David was placed over a thousand men and went out to battle. He was successful in battle and continued to find favor with the People.

David's success continued to trouble Saul and, heeding Satan's whispering, he became fearful of David. Satan took advantage of Saul's fear. He whispered to him, "You must do something about his boy. He will soon have enough support to challenge you to be king. Offer him your daughter that he might be family and not threaten you."

"But he is a poor boy without the bride price." Answered Saul.

"Exactly!" Answered Satan. "If you attack David directly the People will be upset, since they love David. But tell him you will accept the foreskin of one hundred Philistines as the bride price. He will surely fail, they will kill him for you, and you will find favor with your People again. They cannot but support the king as he grieves the loss of his commander and future son-in-law."

Satan's words made sense to Saul and he did as Satan suggested. To Saul's and Satan's chagrin, David returned with the foreskins and presented them to Saul. Saul, reluctantly gave his daughter Michal to be David's wife.

"A woman shall leave her father and love her husband," I thought. "Unfortunate!" I said to Satan.

Everything Saul contrived to undermine David failed. David continued to be successful in battle and was esteemed by the People and other men. Threatened by the success and urged on by Satan, Saul's desire to kill David became so enflamed that David fled to save his life.

In Hell Satan pace back and forth and pondered his options aloud. "This Saul, has clearly lost the favor of the Lord, he acknowledged it and showed us Samuel anointing the boy David. Yet my efforts to encourage Saul to kill David have been ineffective."

"Not just ineffective but they have helped to make the shepherd boy a great warrior." I thought. I said, "We know that the Lord has anointed this David. But he has not seen fit to raise him up."

"What of it?" Satan sneered.

"You have tasked me to watch and record. What use you give to my information is of your concern." I said, more boldly than I intended.

"That's it!" Satan exclaimed. "We will get him to take the kingdom prematurely, and not in the Lord's time. That will cause him to fall out of favor with the Lord and be rejected as king too."

Satan contrived the circumstances to deliver Saul into David's hands. Once when Saul was in pursuit of David, David entered into camp under cover of night. Satan whispered to him. "Here is your enemy, pin him to the ground and the People will make you king."

But David would not listen. Instead he took Saul's spear and water jug saying, "God forbid that I should take the life of the Lord's anointed. When the time comes for him to die, either in battle or old age; that is the Lord's decision." He took the spear and jug across the ravine and called out to Saul and his troops. First he rebuked Saul's entourage for failing to protect him, then he spoke to Saul. "Here is the king's spear. Although he has delivered you into my hands, I could not lay a finger on the Lord's anointed. Just as I regarded your life as sacred, may the Lord regard my life as sacred and deliver me from all danger."

I smiled as I watched Satan come to the realization that his plan had not only failed but had led to David having the assurance that the Lord would hold his life sacred and deliver him from all harm.

In the end, Saul recognized that he had lost all favor of the Lord, yet he still sought the favor of the People. He and his son died in battle against the Philistines on the same day, making room for the ascension of David to the throne. Satan tried to cause division between the People, (It was a tactic he used with greater success later in the People's history.) encouraging Saul's commander, Abner, to declare Ishbaal, Saul's son, as king. But David, ultimately with Abner's help, was able to consolidate his power and was declared king over all the People at Hebron.

Once David had consolidated his power and made king over all the People, Satan directed his efforts to stir up the nations against Israel. David, with the Lord's help, was able to put an end to the strife. As a result, David turned his attention to plans to build a temple. But God, through his prophet Nathan, told David that the construction of the temple would not be for him but would be done by his son.

Despite David's success, Satan would not rest his efforts to bring about the destruction of God's Chosen People. It so happened that Nahash, the king of the Ammonites, died. Because of Nahash's previous kindness, David sent servants to Hanun, the king's son, to console him. But Satan whispered to the princes of the Ammonites. "Do you not see what will happen? David will make your king his vassal. Hanun will take from you and give to David."

The princes listened to Satan and said to Hanun, "Do not think that David is sending these servants merely to console you for the sake of your father. They are spies! David has made vassals of the Moabites, Arameans, and the Edomites. He has designs to do the same to you."

Satan also whispered to Hanun. "This man sends spies into your territory when you are vulnerable after the death of your beloved father. David may have felt a kindness to your father, but what is that to you? With your father gone he will have no reason to hold back any longer. Send him a message that he will surely understand?"

The young king listened to Satan and his princes and decided to send David a message. So he seized the servants and disgraced them, sending them back to David with half their beards shaven and their garments cut to disclose their buttocks. Once Hanun had disgraced David's servants and sent them on their way Satan began to whisper differently. "Now you've kicked the hornet's nest. David will not allow this disgrace to go unpunished. Hire yourself some mercenaries to protect your kingdom when he comes."

Hanun listened to Satan's whisperings and became fearful. He hired mercenaries from the Arameans as well as from the king of Maacah and from the men of Tob. But David was not deterred. He sent his whole army against the Ammonites and put the mercenaries to flight. The following spring he sent his army to lay siege against Rabbah while he remained behind in Jerusalem.

Satan complained as we watched the king of Israel. "Why does he not go out with his armies? Despite my best efforts he has remained faithful. My hope was that he would be slain in battle."

"*He is a man after God's own heart!*" I thought. "There must be something." I said.

Later we watched as one evening David could not sleep. He went to the roof to look at the sky. He scanned the heights of the city. "Great is the Lord and highly to be praise in the City of our God." He said as he scanned the city. But as he watched his eyes fell upon a woman, beautiful to behold, on a roof in the distance preparing to bathe. As he watched desire rose within him.

"Here is your opportunity." I said to Satan, not really knowing why I would have said it. "David has not heeded Moses' warning about taking multiple wives."

"God gave Flesh this sexual desire, which he refuses to us. 'For their good,' he would no doubt say, but I will use it to their downfall." So Satan whispered to David, "She is beautiful. You are king. Who can deny you?"

David allowed Satan's words to further stir his desires, so he sent servants to inquire concerning the woman. When they returned they told him that her name was Bathsheba, the wife of Uriah.

"She is married, I cannot." David said to himself.

"You are king!" Satan repeated. "Who can deny you?"

"She is the wife of Uriah, my commander's armor bearer." He spoke aloud, not realizing that he was engaged in a conversation.

"She is beautiful and you are king."

David allowed his desire for her to overcome his reservations, so he sent for and slept with her and she became pregnant. When David learned that she was pregnant he devised a scheme where his adultery would not be discovered and Bathsheba would not be dishonored. He sent a message to Joab, his commander, asking that he send Uriah to him under the pretext of learning how the battle was going. It was his plan that once Uriah was home he would sleep with his wife and her pregnancy would then be believed to be from her husband.

Unfortunately for David's plan, Uriah would not leave his men nor sleep in the comfort of his home while the armies were encamped in the battlefield.

When he could not convince Uriah to return to his wife David began to worry. Satan said to me, "You were right, this is the opportunity we were looking for." To David he whispered, "He is a soldier – soldiers die in battle every day. If he were to die Bathsheba could be yours and then you would not have to hide what has happened."

As Satan whispered these words I recalled how many times David had sought the Lord's Will. There had been the time before he had been made king when the Amalekites had attacked a town and carried off its inhabitants, including his own wife. The normal course would have been to pursue them and recapture the spoils. But before doing that, David paused and sought the Lord's Will. I hoped that he would do so now. *"Bless the Lord who pardons all your sins."* I prayed. To Satan I said, "Well said sir."

David did not seek the Lord's counsel and instead sent word to Joab to advance against the Ammonites and leave Uriah exposed at the front. Which Joab did! Uriah was killed by the Ammonites but the guilt for his death lay upon David.

Satan and I returned to the throne room where he taunted the Lord. "This one is a man after your own heart? Are you too an adulterer? Was he the one of who you spoke so long ago?"

But the Lord said, "I am disappointed in my son David, but he was not the one of whom I spoke. If he repents of his sin I will forgive him."

As the Lord said this we heard David cry out "Have mercy on me

God, in accord with your merciful love. In your abundant compassion blot out my transgression …"

The Lord smiled and continued, "But I tell you this, the one of whom I spoke will come from David's line, and by your actions you have made it so. Now be gone!" With that He nodded to Michael but Satan did not need any encouragement to leave the Lord's presence.

When we returned to the fires of Hell where I felt no warmth despite the inferno Satan said, "So at last he has given us a clue. We will disrupt David's line. In doing so we will prevent the one from being born. What do you suppose he meant that I had made it so?" He said aloud to himself.

A HOUSE DIVIDED

fter that Satan concentrated his efforts on the line of David. He incited jealousies and intrigue through generation upon generation until the kingdom was wrenched from the line during the exile. Afterwards the People would have a king, but it would be a puppet king put in place by the countries that ruled over them. Satan was convinced that he had defeated God's plan. Although I hated to admit it, I feared the same thing. I prayed, "Remember O Lord for David and all his hardships." As I prayed, I heard the voice of the Lord: "That Lord has made everything for a purpose, even the wicked for the evil days." I need not record them all here (they are available elsewhere.) But I will briefly mention several of them as it suits my purpose.

We were back in Hell and Satan was sitting on his makeshift throne muttering. "The Lord continues to fight for this People. He sends Michael to fight for them. There must be a way."

"A house divided cannot stand!" I said out of nowhere.

"What?" Satan asked, interrupted from his mutterings.

"I – I just said a house divided cannot stand."

"That's it!" Satan beamed. With that idea, he attempted to create division as David neared death. He encouraged the ambition of Adonijah, one of David's sons. Adonijah had chariots and horse assembled and gathered around him a court of his own. He gained favor with a number of David's officials. When the time was right Satan urged him to sacrifice a number of holocausts ("for that is what kings do." Satan had told him) and gathered his brothers, and the royal officials of Judah in a bid to be declared king upon David's death.

But Solomon's mother, Bathsheba, learned of the plot and went to David to remind him of the promise made to her regarding Solomon. At her urgings David arranged for Solomon to be anointed and declared king. At the time I thought *"Once again confounded by a woman."*

Solomon's reign as king was, by all accounts successful. He build the temple to the Lord as the Lord had promised David. Yet he failed to heed the warnings that had been given by Moses regarding the conduct of the king. He accumulate vast fortunes and took a number of wives from the surrounding nations. "David secured the kingdom, and Solomon built the temple, but let us remind the People of the hardships that a king imposes." He had said as he attempted to use these entanglements to destroy the People.

When the time had come for Solomon to pass on the kingship we watched as Solomon called his son Rehoboam. He said his to son, "Your grandfather, my father, King David was a man of war. With the Lord's help he waged war to extend the kingdom which I am about to give you. For my part, God has given me wisdom through which I have secured the kingdom which my father presented to me. I fear that neither war nor wisdom alone will be sufficient to protect your kingdom. Listen well to the men who have counseled me, for they have gained wisdom in my service." Turning to the old men, Solomon continued, "Rehoboam is now your king!"

With his plan to drive a wedge between the People, Satan stirred up the northern tribes. "Do you not notice that all the contributions you have made resulted in a palace and a temple in Judah?" His voice filled with scorn as he said Judah. "And on top of all this you must also provide for the royal household. What has it gotten you?

The leaders of Israel listened to Satan and sent a delegation to Rehoboam. They said to him, "Your father laid a heavy burden on us. If you lift part of that burden we will accept you as our king."

Rehoboam, mindful of his father's words, and wishing to show wisdom like his father, told the men to wait three days so he could consider the matter. He sought out the advice of his father's counselors as instructed. They told him, "If you do as they require today, they will be your servants forever."

But Satan, wishing to bring discord, whispered to him, "You need not be tied to the past. Consult your own counsel." To the younger men, whom Rehoboam surrounded himself with, Satan whispered, "You get your status through the power of the king. If he appears weak by giving in to this crowd, your position will be weakened. It is obvious that the contribution was not too burdensome, for they did not complain against Solomon. Besides, their contribution goes to the King's household. Certainly you want more rather than less?"

So they said to Rehoboam, "This is your first test. If you give into them, all those you collect tribute from will also seek a reduction. You must appear strong so others will not approach you to lift their burdens. Tell them 'you think my father's yoke was heavy, my little finger is thicker than my father's loins. I will make your yoke heavier. He beat you with whips, I will beat you with scorpions.'"

Rehoboam listened to the advice of his younger counselors and when the delegation from Israel returned on the third day, he told them all that they had suggested.

Satan continued his attack on the People of God, driving the wedge between them deeper. Once Rehoboam sent out the man in charge of forced labor to the north. Satan whispered to them, "Here is the man in charge of forced labor. Rehoboam still intends to assert his authority over you. Send him a clear message that you will not bow to him." Roused by his words, the People stoned the man.

When the news of what had happened to his man reached Rehoboam, Satan whispered to him, "You see, they have totally rejected you as their king. They are no different than any other of your vassals. Go out to war (for that is what kings do!) and bring them under your control." Rehoboam listened to Satan and assembled the house of Judah and the Benjaminites for war. But the word of the Lord came to him through the prophet Shemaiah that he must not go to war with the northern tribes. He heeded the word of the Lord and turned back from the attack.

Back in Hell Satan fumed over the fact that his plan had failed. "It's as if the Lord condones this rivalry between the People."

I thought so too, but then considered that if Rehoboam had attached the northern tribes, the rift may have become permanent. "Maybe the Lord will tolerate a short-term division?"

"That must be it!" He answered, and returned to earth to continue his efforts to make the division permanent.

"You have done well to sever your ties to Jerusalem . . ." At that thought, the king appeared startled. Satan, realizing his mistake spoke quickly. "Jerusalem is just a place that David favored, it is nothing special."

But the king spoke aloud, "It is the place where the People go to worship the Lord."

"That is true." Admitted Satan. "If the People go up to Jerusalem, their hearts will return to Rehoboam and he will kill you. The People worshiped the Lord forty years in the desert did they not? Set up places for them here in the north. Make golden calves and present them to the People. They will be their gods and they will no longer need to go to Jerusalem. Otherwise, you might as well return and subjugate yourself to the King of Judah." Satan stirred up thoughts in the man's mind of the turmoil he would suffer if the People returned to Jerusalem. Fearful of these thoughts, he set up places of worship in the north as Satan had suggested.

After this, the two kingdoms continued, side by side each raising up kings for themselves and it appeared that Satan's plan to destroy their idea of what a king would be was working. Although there were some kings that did what was pleasing in God's sight, many did not. Ahaz was one of those kings that refused to follow the Lord.

Satan, not content with his plan to sully the idea of a king in the People's mind, roused the king of Aram to come against Judah. Ahaz, sought help from the King of Assyria rather than the Lord. So the Lord, sent his prophet Isaiah to speak to him.

"You need not seek the assistance of the Assyrians. Simply return to the God of your fathers and he will deliver you." Counseled Isaiah.

"He did not preserve the kingdom of Israel. You know for yourself how many of its fortified cities have already fallen. Pekah joined with the Arameans in their latest efforts to unseat you. He will not be able to save you!" Satan whispered.

Isaiah, apparently able to understand the whisperings of Satan said, "That is not true! "Ask for a sign from the Lord. It can be whatever you want, as deep as Sheol or as high as the sky. Then you will know that the Lord is capable to do all that he says."

But Satan whispered, "You know the Law. You should not put the Lord to the test."

"How hypocritical that this one who has opposed the Lord so openly would quote the law." I thought, but I said. "Do you think it wise to quote the Law? This king has abandoned the Law his entire reign."

"I will not tempt the Lord!" Said Ahaz.

Satan looked at me with satisfaction and left. He did not hear Isaiah continue. "Since you refuse to ask for a sign, know that the Lord himself will give you a sign. A young woman shall give birth to a son and call him Emmanuel. The child will come to know to reject evil and choose what is good. Before that time however, the two kingdoms which have been set up shall be destroyed."

Ahaz refused to rely on the Lord and went to Assyria with the temple gold as tribute. While there he saw the altar which had been set up in Damascus. Satan was there and whispered, "See what a glorious altar. Compared to this, the altar on which you offer sacrifice to your God is like a trough for feeding animals. No wonder the Assyrians are so powerful, why there god has enabled them to conquer the world. Make an altar like this and offer sacrifice to their god."

Satan's words seemed wise to Ahaz and that's what he did.

It was not long after this that the king of Assyria came and invaded the Northern Kingdom. He deported the People, dispersing them throughout his kingdom. In their place he sent people from the regions of Babylon, Cuthah, Avva, Hamath, and Sepharvaim to dwell there. It seemed to me the reversal of what the Lord had done for his Chosen People at the time of the Exodus. Then he cleared the nations from Canaan to make room for them. Now the People have been driven out and others have been brought in.

THE LORD CAN SAVE

ow Satan continued his attack on the Israelites. He was not satisfied that the Jews had been captured and that Jeconiah, the king of Judah, and his People had been exiled to Babylon. It was his desire to see the People destroyed. Only then could he be assured that the one of whom God spoke would not come. In time he learned of a Jew named Mordecai who lived in Susa under the reign of King Ahasuerus.

King Ahasuerus had taken a lenient view towards the Jews and tolerated them in his kingdom. Nevertheless, Satan looked for ways to make the Jews suffer. To Satan's chagrin a Jewess named Ester had found favor with the king and had been named queen. So Satan decided he should be rid of King Ahasuerus in order to raise up a king that would not be so accommodating. He inspired two of the king's eunuchs to assassinate Ahasuerus.

Mordecai became aware of the plot and informed his niece Ester, the queen. Ester in turn made it known to the king that a man named Mordecai had discovered the plot. Upon investigation it was found to be true and the eunuchs were executed. Following the tradition of men (and not too much different from Satan's plan for me) the entire episode, including Mordecai's involvement, was reported in something called The Book of Memorable Deeds. Afterwards Satan redoubled his efforts to destroy the Jews. He paid special attention to Mordecai because of his interference with the assassination plot.

Satan in his scheming learned of a man named Haman who was ambitious and thought to use this ambition to his advantage. So we approached the throne room of the king and Satan whispered to him,

"Do you see that man Haman? He is an ambitious one. You can use that ambition to serve you or it may overcome you."

"I will have him killed." The king responded without knowing to whom he was speaking.

"No that will not work. If you do so, someone will simply take his place. Instead, raise him up – put him at your right hand then he will cherish his place and make sure that none will take it."

This advice seemed good to Ahasuerus so he promoted Haman and set him above all the other advisers. Satan whispered to Ahasuerus, "Command that all lesser servants must bow down to Haman to give him homage."

The similarity to Satan's position seemed uncanny. He was created to sit at the feet of the Lord, higher than any of the other angels. He sought homage that was due only to the Lord. I hoped Ahasuerus would see through Satan's advice, but I said, "That is a good idea."

"Why should anyone receive homage but me?" Asked Ahasuerus.

"Homage to one who gives you homage is just like homage to you." Satan lied. In the end Ahasuerus did as Satan suggested and ordered that Haman be given homage.

It was Satan's intention to use this command to bring down Modecai. One day Haman was at the king's gate and all the other officials bowed down to give him homage according to the king's command. While all the others bowed to Haman, Mordecai alone remained upright. His companions took note of Mordecai's posture and heard Satan whisper, "Look at Mordecai! He thinks he is better than you. He does not bow as commanded by the kings."

The men queried Mordecai regarding his refusal to pay homage.

"I am an exile from the land of Judah. I mean no disrespect to Haman, nor do I disregard the king's authority over me in other matters, but my homage is due to the Lord alone."

Each day as Haman passed the men bowed while Mordecai stood upright. Satan again whispered to the men, "Maybe he knows something that you do not. He is playing you for a fool as you bow to Haman. He is not king!"

"If only you heard yourself, if they could hear how you contradict yourself." I thought.

"Maybe the command has been rescinded." Satan continued.

"That could not be possible." One of the men remarked. "Once it is written in the book of the king it may not be rescinded."

"Ask Haman!" Satan whispered, knowing that it had not been rescinded. "He will know."

The men did as Satan suggested and were assured by Haman that the command had not been rescinded. They recounted how day after day Mordecai stands at the gate and does not pay homage as Haman passes by.

"What reason does the man give for his refusal?" Asked Haman, trying to hold his anger.

"He is a Jew and says that he and his People pay homage to their God alone."

Upon hearing this, Haman flew into a rage and vowed that he would make Mordecai pay for his dishonor. Satan fueled Haman's rage whispering, "Who is this man who refuses you honor? His entire race is a threat to you."

Satan continued his taunting until Haman finally asked, "What shall I do?"

"Go to the king and warn him about this People. Tell him they must be destroyed."

"But I've checked. This People are dispersed throughout the entire kingdom in every province. The king will never allow that many people to be destroyed."

"Offer to pay him." I suggested.

"Offer him 10,000 talents of silver." Said Satan, as if it was his own idea.

"10,000 talents!" Haman exclaimed in shock. "Would I spend 10,000 talents to punish his refusal?"

"Is not your honor worth that?" Satan asked. "Besides, would you not spend that if you could get much more than that in return?"

"I am listening." He replied.

Satan continued. "This People have grown prosperous during their exile in your land. Once they are destroyed to whom should their goods be delivered?"

So Haman appeared in the presence of the king and said, "There is a People exiled from another land living throughout your kingdom. Despite enjoying the protection of your laws, they maintain the law from where they have come, even those in conflict with your laws. It is not good that they be allowed to ignore your laws or keep their own. What would happen if all the foreigners chose to obey the laws of their country rather than yours?"

"What would you suggest asked the King?"

"Let it be decreed that this People be destroyed throughout your kingdom and I will pay 10,000 talents in silver into the king's treasury."

The king gave his signet ring to Haman, along with the permission to do as he had proposed. Satan returned to Hell confident that he had found the means to destroy the Israelites, the Lord's Beloved.

For my part, I wondered what would become of them. I pondered. *"You have sold your People for a trifle, demanding no high price for them. Awake! Why are you sleeping, O Lord? Rouse yourself do not reject your People forever."*

So Haman did what he proposed and had an order issued in the king's name for the destruction of the Israelites. When Mordecai, along with all the Jews throughout the kingdom, learned of it he went into mourning. He tore his clothes and put on sackcloth and ashes.

When Ester learned of Mordecai's actions she sent one of her eunuchs, Hathach, to find out what had happened. Mordecai related to Hathach all that Haman had ordered and gave him a copy of the decree. He asked him to relay these things to Ester and to give her a copy of the order. Mordecai told the Eunuch to ask Ester to go to the king and pleaded for her People.

Satan watched with delight (if he was capable of that emotion) at Mordecai's distress as he considered the prospect of the destruction of the Jews.

"The King's prediction will come to nothing." Satan crowed.

"Why do you boast of evil?" I thought. *"God will break you down forever."* I said, "Most assuredly."

We watched Hathach as he related to Ester all that Mordecai had said.

Satan whispered to Ester, "You cannot do what Mordecai asks! You know that should you approach the king unbidden, you will surely die.

You need not worry though. Certainly the order will not apply to you. Why risk death for a People you do not know, from a land you have never been."

I wanted to scream out, "*Behold God is your helper; The Lord is the upholder of life. He will return the evil to your enemies. In your faithfulness put an end to them.*" But I said nothing as we left her there trembling. It was apparent that Satan's words had their intended effect. She asked Hathach to relay her fears to Mordecai.

When Mordecai heard her response he said to Hathach, "Tell her – Do not think to yourself that in the king's palace you will escape any more than all the other Jews. For if you keep silent at this time, I have no doubt that relief and deliverance will rise from another place, but you and your father's house will perish."

Hathach relayed Mordecai's warning to Ester. Upon considering his words she told Hathach, "Tell Mordecai to gather all the Jews and hold a fast on my behalf. Do not eat or drink for three days or nights. Then I will go to the king though it be against the law, I will take the risk."

After the third day Ester put on her royal robes and went before the king. "The Lord gives power to the faint and strength to the weak," she said as she left her chambers. She opened the door and entered. The room was appropriately adorned to reflect the royal state. There was a wide open space between the chamber doors and the dais upon which the king sat. As she entered the palace guards drew their weapons and stood between her and the king. Ahasuerus looked up and saw his queen and motioned to allow her to approach.

"You risk much coming here unbidden my queen. It must be important. What is your request?"

"If it please the king, let me prepare a feast today for yourself and Haman."

The king assented to Ester's request, still wondering what has been so important. Later, as the king and Haman ate and drank he became more intrigued with Ester's motivation. Gladdened by the wine he asked, "What is your request? Even up to half my kingdom, it shall be granted."

"If I have found favor with you my king – let me prepare yet another feast for you and Haman tomorrow and then I shall tell you my request."

Said Ester with a slight bow as she captured the king with her eyes. The king assented to her request and invited Haman to join him again the following night.

We returned to Hell as Satan fumed. "What is that Jewess planning? I cannot allow her to interfere with my plan. What is my next move?"

"Mordecai!" I exclaimed, regretting it as soon as I spoke it.

"Explain!"

"Mordecai gives her strength and advice do not allow her to consult him."

Excellent idea, I will arrange to have him killed in the morning, before she has a chance to consult him."

We watched as Haman left the palace for home, walking chin high and proud. "Who else has been invited for a feast with the king, not once but twice?" He said to himself as he approached the king's gate. He took pride as the men there bowed as he passed – all but Mordecai.

"Look at that Jew!" Satan whispered. "Despite your order he continues to defy you. You have been honored by a feast with the king. Do not wait for the scheduled date for the destruction of all his People. Take advantage of your position with the king and have him killed tomorrow morning."

When he returned to his home Zeresh, his wife, anxious to hear about his feast with the king, asked how it went. He told her of his evening as Satan's words burned within him. "And tomorrow I am invited to a second feast, but all this is nothing if that Mordecai continues to sit at the gate. Soon others will begin to follow his example and all will be lost."

"What is better?" Satan whispered to Zeresh, "to be married to the king's right hand man or, to one of the king's many counselors?"

Spurred on by Satan's words, she spoke. "Rid yourself of this man. Build yourself a gibbet and ask the king for his head in the morning."

He didn't ordinarily like his wife getting involved with his affairs, but her words coincided with what he had thought as he walked home. He ordered a gibbet to be erected in front of his home.

Satan returned to Hell satisfied that he had brought down Mordecai and would soon see the destruction of the entire race. It would mean the downfall of the Lord's prediction. He either did not notice or care that

I lingered. I went to Mordecai at the King's Gate. He sat in the dust wearing sackcloth praying for the Lord's instructions. I went to Ester's chambers and listened to her prayer as well.

"O God, I have heard of your deeds of old. How your hand drove out the nations. But now you have rejected us. You have made us the taunt of our neighbors, the derision and scorn of those around us. Awake! Why are you sleeping? Rouse yourself! Do not reject us forever."

Instantly, I was transported to the chambers of King Ahasuerus. He suddenly awoke and could not return to sleep. And then it hit me, I had been created to watch and report. As reported earlier, the time when Mordecai had saved the king had been recorded in The Book of Memorable Deeds. As, I recalled this the king asked that the book be brought to him and for his attendant to read from the book. When they got to the assassination attempt thwarted by Mordecai the king asked what had been done for him.

"Nothing is reported here sir." Replied the attendant.

King Ahasuerus was surprised and asked who is in the court.

I returned to Hell, confident that the Lord had saved Mordecai, yet wondered how He would save his People. "Something is happening in the King's chambers." I said to Satan and we returned to earth in time to see Haman entering the court.

"It is good that you recalled us here. There is Haman, going to ask the king permission to put Mordecai on the gibbet."

As we watched, we heard the king's attendant tell him that Haman had just entered the court.

"Have him come in!" Ordered the king.

Haman entered the court, but before he could ask about Mordecai, the king asked, "What should be done to the man whom the king wishes to honor?"

Satan, believing it time for Haman to press his advantage, whispered, "He must be talking about you. Now is the time to make your request."

Haman, thought to himself, *"Who would the king delight to honor more than me?"* So he said, "For the man whom the king delights to honor, let royal robes worn by the king himself be brought, and a horse ridden by the king be brought and a royal crown and place upon his head. Adorned in such a manner, let him be led through the city on the horse while proclaiming "Thus shall it be done to the man whom the kings delights to honor."

"Well said!" Exclaimed the king. "Take the robe, crown and the horse as you have said . . ."

At this moment Haman realized that the king had not been thinking of him when he asked the question. He did not however, let his disappointment show. Satisfied, at least that the king had thought highly enough to ask his opinion and had approved it, he asked, "To whom should they be given?"

"To Mordecai, the Jew who sits at the king's gate."

"To Mordecai?" Haman stammered.

"Yes!" Exclaimed the king. "He uncovered and disclosed an assassination plot and has not yet been rewarded. Now go and do as you have said."

I watched with some enjoyment as Haman dressed Mordecai in the king's robes and led him through the streets upon the king's horse all the while wearing the king's crown.

Haman seethed as he declared, "Thus shall it be done to the man whom the king delights to honor."

I heard Mordecai silently pray, "I know that God is for me. In God I trust. I will render thanks offerings to you."

When Haman returned home he was bitter and sorrowful. For Satan's part, he cared little for Haman's distress. Haman was just a pawn in his battle against the King. His hatred for the People whom God had chosen was all consuming. It blinded him of the realities. Haman's friends however, gave him an ominous warning. "If this Mordecai is a Jew you will not overcome him but will surely fall before him."

Before Haman could reply the king's eunuch arrived to take him to the feast Ester had prepared. As on the previous night the feast consisted of fine food and wine. Not being Flesh, I cannot do justice in my description, but there was every kind of fruit, bread and cheese, meat from the herd and spiced wine. After the food had been cleared and the king and Haman sat enjoying their wine, the King asked Ester about her request. "Even to half of my kingdom, it shall be fulfilled." Finished the king, as he had said the night before.

Ester bowed before the king and said, "If I have found favor with the king let my life be granted for my wish, and the life of my People for my request."

The king looked puzzled, Haman, recalling his friends' warning earlier, looked fearful. Ester continued, "For my People and I have been sold to be destroyed. It is not even that we have been sold as slaves. If that had been true I would have been quiet, though the king would suffered more by the loss."

"Who would dare sell an entire People?" Asked the king?

"He is an enemy of the king!" She replied.

"Who is he? Where is?" Demanded the king.

"This man, Haman is the one!"

Enraged, the king left the room and went to the palace garden. He gave orders to Harbon, one of his eunuchs, to go to Haman's house to see if there was any truth to Ester's story. Haman remained behind to plead for his life from Ester.

When the king returned to his chambers he saw Haman on the couch impleading with the Queen. "Will you even assault the Queen in my presence? What shall I do with you?"

Harbon returned and reported, "Haman has indeed erected a gibbet upon which he intends to place Mordecai, the very man you have honored today."

"Hang him on it!" The King ordered.

With that we left. Satan was not concerned with Haman's fate. He knew that the Lord had once again sheltered his People. *"Like a mother bird sheltering her offspring beneath her wings."* I thought.

ANOTHER DEFEAT

here was another time, after the People had returned from their exile (The details of their exile and the return are available elsewhere.) where Satan attempted to stir up the politics of the day as a means to rid the world of the Jewish People, and by doing so thwart the will of God. At a time when Nebuchadnezzar was at battle with King Arphaxad of Media, he desired to bring support from his vassals in Persia including Israel. He sent an order commanding that they join him, which the People of God refused to follow.

Satan roused the King of the Assyrians and whispered to him, "It is not right that your reign has not reached into Persia. Your strength and majesty are renowned even there, yet they do not give you homage and keep your commands." Satan's words struck a chord with Nebuchadnezzar but he was focused on his conquest.

After some time he was able to defeat Arphaxad without the help of the western vassals. He returned home with the spoils of victory, but Satan did not let him forget the earlier spurn of the western nations. "Why do you let the kings of the West brag how they ignored your command? If it becomes known, will not the other vassal nations refuse your command and fail to give you homage?" He said to the king.

Finally, after some time (as I have said time has no meaning for us, as we are eternal being so Satan could be patient with the king.) Nebuchadnezzar called in his counselors and told them of his secret plan for reprisal on the Western Nations.

He commissioned Holofernes, his highest ranking commander, to carry out the first steps of his plan. He said, "Go ahead of me throughout the lands of the West. If they surrender to you, keep them secure until I come following you to render judgment. If they refuse to surrender, then you shall slaughter them and plunder their land."

So Holofernes assembled a massive force and led his army out in advance of King Nebuchadnezzar. The first of the cities he reached he utterly destroyed. As his progress west continued, the nations came out and sued for peace.

But Satan, hoping that his ravaging would continue all the way to Israel whispered to him. "See the people claim they wish to submit to your king – but look at them. Sacred groves and the gods they have set up for themselves. Ride through their nation and destroy them so that they may worship none but your king." Satan's words sounded good to Holofernes and that's what he did.

So as he passed through the lands he laid waste to the sacred places of the people whose land he conquered. He reached the mountains near a place called Bethulia through which he must pass to enter into Judea and stopped there to rest and resupply his army.

Although Satan paid no heed, I noticed that the People of Israel cried out to the Lord God. All the while preparing themselves for battle. Satan, for his part, was more concerned with the Assyrian war council. We watched as Holofernes learned that the Israelites alone of all the people had readied themselves for battle. Achior, the leader of the Ammonites spoke. We listened as he recounted the history of the Israelites from Abraham through the escape from Egypt and their conquest of Canaan. He concluded, "As long as the Israelites did not sin in the sight of their God, they prospered. But when they sinned against him – they were utterly destroyed. Your way then is clear. If they have sinned and we can verify it – attack and you will be successful. But if not, then do not attack because you cannot possibly prevail!"

"Not so!" Satan lied. "Look at the size of your army. They are a powerless People. Incapable of a strong defense. They will become fodder for your great army." Satan urged the surrounding nations that had suffered much from the Israelites to join him in his encouragement of Holofernes. They too urged him to attack. "Besides," Satan added, "this is a stiff necked People. It is likely that there is sin amongst them."

Holofernes was emboldened by Satan's words and spoke to Achior. "Who are you to speak to us like that? Who is god besides

Nebuchadnezzar? He will send his army and destroy this People from the face of the earth. Their God cannot save them!" Pulling Achior closer, he said "As for you, you will not see my face after today until I have taken my revenge on this People. After that I will have you killed."

Satan was pleased that Holofernes had so readily listened to his council so he whispered again. "Do not allow this man to remain in your midst. Did you not see how his words made some of your men quake? His words will poison your ranks. Have him taken to the city where he will be killed along with all the inhabitants."

Satan's words sounded good to Holofernes so he continued, "Now I will have you delivered into their midst. You shall not die until you are slaughtered along with them. If you have any hope that their God will save them," he taunted, "then you have nothing to worry about."

We watched as Holofernes' men led Achior away. They led him outside the town of Bethulia where they bound him and left him lying there. The men of Bethulia drove Holofernes' men away and went to the gates to bring Achior into the city. We watched as he relayed all that had been said and done.

We returned to the Assyrian camp and watched as Holofernes prepared his troops for battle. While in Bethulia the sheer size of the army made the Israelites tremble. Nevertheless, they took up their arms and prepared to defend themselves. The next day Holofernes led out his cavalry in the hopes of causing fear and surrender. When that did not occur he used the time to reconnoiter the area. He located the springs that served as the city's water source and seized them, setting guards to secure them.

When he returned to his camp we watched as the rulers of the surrounding nations came to caution him. "These People do not rely on their weapons as a normal army does. They hide out and take advantage of the terrain. If you would like our counsel you can take the city without any loss of your men."

"Continue!" He commanded.

"Take some men and close the flow of their water." Holofernes smirked because he had already ordered that to be done. They continued, "Their thirst will cause them to surrender. We will take our men to the other side to see that none will escape."

"I have already seized the water supply, but you take your men and see that none escapes."

We watched as the siege continued for nearly three weeks. (Although for us time has no meaning.) We watched as the reservoirs within the city dried up. The women and children were the first to show signs of dehydration as they became listless, collapsing in the streets. Satan saw the hardship caused by the siege and began to whisper to the People. "Your God has sold you like sheep for the slaughter."

I thought, "*Though an enemy encamps against you, do not allow your heart to fear.*"

"Vassals of the Assyrians would be better than dying of thirst." Satan continued his torment. The People listened to Satan's whispering and pleaded with the town's rulers to surrender.

Uzziah, the High Priest urged the People not to lose hope. But Satan whispered to him, "You are a hypocrite for as you call them to hope you too begin to doubt. How much longer would you expect them to wait? You are his priest, demand that he answer within the next five days if not, then know that he has abandoned you?"

I thought, "*Do not put the Lord your God to the test.*" And prayed that God would give the priest wisdom.

In the end, the priest did something in between Satan's whispering, and my prayers. He acknowledged his doubt but he was not so bold to demand anything from the Lord. Instead he simply told the People to wait another five days and if the Lord had not answered by then, he would allow them to surrender.

Now unbeknownst to Satan there was a widow in the city from the tribe of Manasseh whose name was Judith. Why Satan was unaware of her when he seemed to know so much, I did not then understand. But I thought, "Maybe she is the one who is to become the Most Favored." While Satan watched the preparations for war by the Assyrians, I watched as she summoned the rulers of the city and Uzziah. I watched as she chastised them. "Who are you to test the Lord by placing deadlines on his actions? If it is not his plan to come to our aid in five days have no doubt that he has it in his power to protect us until he chooses to act."

She continued, "You yourselves know that unlike in the past we have kept ourselves from sinning. We have not taken foreign gods in our midst, God will not fail us. Besides if we should fall, all of Judea, including the Temple, will fall. Let us set ourselves as an example to our kinsmen. He has tested our ancestors in the past – do not think that this has happened as vengeance, but rather to try us like gold is tested in fire."

The rulers of the city and the High Priest were embarrassed by her words. Uzziah was first to speak. "We know your words are true and we trust your counsel now, but the People were so thirsty that we gave an oath that we cannot now take back. Since you are a devout woman, pray for us and maybe God well send rain."

Judith responded, "Listen I will do something that will be remembered for generations to come. Let me pass through the gate tonight and do not inquire of my plan. But within the time you have made your oath to the People, the Lord will deliver Israel by my hand."

"Go in peace." They said to her, "and may the Lord take vengeance on our enemies."

As they left her tent, I returned to Satan. "Where have you been?" He asked.

"You have asked me to watch. While you took note of the battle preparations, I kept watch over the Israelites. Satan turned to me, only slightly interested. "There is a woman," I hesitated. "She has a plan."

"A woman?" Satan scoffed.

"Remember that he had said the one to replace you as Most Favored." I hesitated as I saw Satan cringe. "Would be a woman."

"Yes! But what could she do to an army?"

"I don't know sir, she would not tell the council, but I thought you should know."

"We need not fear a woman." Satan mocked. "But it will be good fun to watch."

So we watched as she prepared to carry out her plan. She had been wearing sackcloth because she had been mourning the loss of her husband. We watched as she put ashes upon her head and prepared to pray.

"What is she saying?" Asked Satan. "I cannot hear!"

"It is strange sir," I said, not letting on that I could hear her.

"Dear Lord, you are author of all things. The present and future you have planned. The Assyrians come against us trusting in shield and spear and bow. They do not know you nor that you are the Lord that crushes armies. Shatter them with your might. Give me a widow, a strong hand to execute my plan. Forgive my deceit but may it defeat those who come against us. Then they will know that you are with us as they have been brought down by the hands of a woman."

When she had finished her prayer she got up and cleaned herself. She set aside the clothes of mourning, anointed herself with fragrant oils, and adorned herself with splendid jewelry. She prepared a simple meal of wine and oil, along with some roasted grain, dried figs, and bread. We watched as she, along with her maid, left the city.

"Perhaps they have grown tired of their thirst and no longer wish to wait upon the Lord." Guessed Satan. "Or maybe, she has been sent to plead for the lives of the women and children."

In any event, she marched straight across the valley and did not hesitate when a patrol approached and took her into custody. She said to them, "I am a Jew and have come to speak to your commander Holofernes. When I speak to him," she paused to emphasize that she would only speak to him. "I will give him a trustworthy report whereby he can take possession without the loss of a single man."

So the leader of the patrol unit ordered that she be accompanied to the tent of Holofernes. We watched as they congregated around her as her message was being related to Holofernes.

"The idiots!" Satan bellowed. "They are being taken in by her beauty." He heard one of the men say, "What is so bad about a People whose women look like this?" So Satan whispered, "It is not good that even one man should be left alive. For if any were spared then through their women, they could beguile the whole world."

When Holofernes was told by the patrol leader of Judith's intentions he called for her to be brought in. When she saw him she fell prostrate before him. We watched as his attendant raised her up and Holofernes assured her that no harm would come to her. "What is it that you have to say?"

After much flattery she told him. "The words spoken by Achior to your council were correct. It is true that the sword cannot prevail against them except when they have sinned against God. But have no fear, their sin has caught up with them. In their hunger they have decided to eat those animals forbidden by God. They have agreed to enter and eat the first fruits of grain that is reserved for the priests. When they have done these things they will be handed over to you. As soon as I became aware of this plan I fled. Allow me to go each night to the valley and pray. When I have learned that they have done as they have planned I will come back and tell you. So that you may go into battle and be successful."

"See – see what I told you earlier." Satan bragged to Holofernes. "It is impossible for any man to keep the law perfectly. God alone could do so. Do as the woman suggests."

Holofernes showed her to a room where she could eat. She refused his offer and chose instead to eat the food she had brought, emphasizing the importance of keeping the dietary laws. After she had eaten she was led to a tent where she could sleep. We watched as she rose in the middle of the night. She sent word to Holofernes to allow her to leave camp and pray, which he granted. Once outside the camp she bathed to purify herself and offered prayers to the Lord. Neither I nor Satan could hear her prayers. She followed this pattern for three nights.

On the fourth day Holofernes was anxious for the conquest to begin. He held a banquet for his servants, intentionally not inviting any of his officers. As the party progressed, Satan whispered to him. "The conquest need not wait. Take the Hebrew woman." He listened to Satan and instructed his personal servant to persuade Judith to join him. Which she did. Judith joined her servant girl who had gone ahead and had spread out a fleece opposite Holofernes to allow Judith to recline there. Holofernes encouraged her to join the feast saying, "Drink and be happy with us."

She replied, "I will gladly drink, for today is the greatest day of my life." Taking what she had brought with her she ate and drank in Holofernes' presence.

Beguiled by her beauty and charms, Holofernes drank more than he was accustomed. As it grew late his servants withdrew from the tent while his personal servant closed the tent and dismissed the attendant in order to give his master some privacy. Judith instructed her maidservant to wait outside the bedchamber in order to join her later to pray.

We watched as Holofernes lay sprawled out on the bed. Despite his efforts it was clear that Holofernes would have no conquest tonight. Instead, we watched as Judith took Holofernes' own sword and after praying for strength lowered the sword and severed his head with two strong blows.

"No" Shouted Satan. "By a woman!"

Judith grabbed the head and placed it into the food bag and handed it to the servant who carried it out of the camp as they had done for the last three nights. Rather than return to the valley to pray, they went up the mountain to Bethulia. As she approached the gate the guards recognized her and ordered that the gate be opened. The entire town came out to hear what had happened while she was away.

"Praise God!" She began. "Praise God for he has not withdrawn his mercy from the house of Israel. He has shattered our enemies by my hand." As she said this she reached into the bag and withdrew the head of Holofernes.

"The harlot slept with man in order to do this." Satan whispered. "She cannot be trusted!"

Though it mattered little to those around her, she felt it important to attest that she had seduced him with her face alone and that she had not been defiled or otherwise sinned. Almost as if answering Satan's accusation.

Satan could no longer stand to hear the People praise God for his wonderful deeds. But before he left he instructed me to watch what happened next. So I watched the next day as Judith proposed that the men prepare for battle and leave the city as if going out to war, but not to engage the Assyrians. She told them "When they see you coming out to battle they will go and wake Holofernes. When they realize that he has been slain in his bed chambers they will panic. Only then shall you attack and strike them down."

The Israelites did as Judith suggested and they destroyed the army and plundered the camp.

I don't know why but there came a time when the Lord seemed to be absent in the lives of this People. Satan seemed to notice it too.

"What is it about this People? What is it about this land? The entire time they were in exile he raised up prophets, but no one who

I suspected to be the one who was the subject of our bet. I must keep the region under foreign rule. Maybe then I can prevent the one from being raised up."

"But if the one is not raised up, you cannot win the bet."

"The bet? Oh yeah! Do you not yet understand? I hate what he loves! The bet is extra."

A CHILD IS BORN

fter the kingdoms had been divided and the People carried off in exile, God sent prophets to them, reminding them of the covenant they had entered and recalling them to faithfulness. During this time, Satan tried to encourage them through various ways to forego the covenant and mingle with the people. Even after they had been allowed to return it seemed that God had forsaken them. Eventually the Romans came and conquered the region. They set up a puppet kingship but left proconsuls over them. I suggested to Satan, "We should return to earth. Something is about to happen!" It was the time of the year when the high priest entered the Holy of Holies. Zechariah was the high priest that year and he was lamenting the fact that he did not have a child.

As we watched an angel appeared and stood to the right of the altar of incense.

"What is he doing here?" Muttered Satan.

"I don't know, but it must be important. It is Gabriel, who stands before God. He must have heard a word from God and has come to share it with the priest."

The angel of God spoke to Zechariah. "Do not be afraid. God has heard your prayers. Your wife Elizabeth will bear a son and you shall name him John. You will have joy and gladness, and many will rejoice at his birth. He will be great in the sight of the Lord be sure that he drinks neither wine nor strong drink. . . ."

"Sounds like Samson." I whispered.

"He will turn many of the children of Israel to the Lord their God." Gabriel continued. But Satan had heard all that he could stand.

I lingered long enough to hear, "He will go before him in the Spirit and power of Elijah. . ."

When I returned to Hell, Satan was pacing back and forth. "Why does he bother with the mechanics of birth anyway?" Satan asked. "He created them from dust, why not continue that way?"

He had asked that question numerous times but it still perplexed him. "*Be fruitful and multiply!*" I remember the Lord's first command to the one named Adam. "*God had decided to allow this new creation to share in his creative work. Although on a different scale, not unlike how he humbled himself to allow angels to share his Glory by assisting this Flesh to become holy. On some level, Satan would recognize the parallel but to mention it would bring ridicule and possibly suspicion.*" Unlike Satan, I was grateful that the Lord has chosen to share his Glory with the angelic hosts. Shaking myself from these thoughts I said: "But he has involved himself in the begetting process of Flesh before." I reminded Satan.

"Yeah, Yeah!" He said, waiving me off, making it clear he wasn't really looking for an answer. But I continued to ponder the notion. Each time the Lord intervened in a special way it seemed to cause a paradigm shift in the life of this People. I realized that something big was about to happen. But simply said, "Remember the woman Sarah?" Whether Satan heard or took note I do not know.

In any event, Satan continued his efforts against this People. On one occasion, we returned from roaming the world and Satan was troubled by the fact that he could not approach a particular woman, a girl really. She was from Bethlehem and betrothed to a man named Joseph. She had taken an oath to the Lord to remain a virgin. Under the law, either her father or husband could revoke the oath without any penalty. Whether her intended would revoke the oath or not, I did not know at the time. In any event, it appeared that she had not been faithful to that oath because she had been found to be pregnant before they had begun to live together. Satan was sure that the discovery of this fact would be the end of their relationship. "He has protected this one, for what? So she could have an illegitimate child? Surely her 'beloved' will put her away." To our surprise, Joseph did not expose her as an adulterer or divorce her, but took her into his home. Satan tried to stir up some of the townspeople to gossip but without success. The woman left the town and went to visit her cousin. Without her presence in the town the gossip soon died out.

The young girl was really a distraction for Satan because he was convinced that John, the boy to be born to Elizabeth, was the one about whom God had spoken. But he could not resolve his doubts. "She is from the house of David. Long forgotten, but still, he must be protecting her for a reason. But it is the one to be named John that I think will be shown to be the one." Satan pondered aloud. "He has waited these 500 of their years without even sending a prophet. Gabriel said he is to turn this People of his back to him."

So we continued to watch his mother, Elizabeth as she became pregnant and prepared to give birth. Two thirds of the way through the pregnancy she was visited by her younger cousin. To Satan and my own surprise it turned out to be the young woman whom we could not approach. We watched their encounter. I was able to hear what they were saying, but Satan could not. Believing that I also could not hear, Satan said, "It must have something to do with his protection of this girl." He left after telling me to keep watch until she left the woman so we could maintain our watch on the developments regarding John who would soon be born.

Satan's lingering doubts required me to split my time between watching Elizabeth and Mary, the woman we could not approach. Shortly after she returned from her visit to her cousin, the authorities ordered a census, which required Joseph to take his wife to his ancestral home, Bethlehem. We watched as Joseph and Mary, who was now quite along in her pregnancy, traveled to Bethlehem. As we watched Satan pondered. "Bethlehem? Why does that backwater town sound so familiar?"

"His prophets once said this 'and you Bethlehem, from you shall come a ruler, who is to shepherd my People.'" I said.

"That's it!" Satan exclaimed. "That is how we will rid ourselves of this distraction. Herod, this puppet king is worse than all the kings of old. Maybe this woman carries a king that is to be the one of whom He spoke." But we soon saw that the man and his wife, arrived not at a villa, but rather they found rest in a stable. The child was born and placed in a manger. Despite these lowly beginnings and questionable parentage,

Satan could not rid himself of the idea that there was something about this boy. His curiosity was further piqued when travelers from the East, apparent royalty, came in search of the boy to deliver him gifts. We learned that they had seen a sign in the stars about the ascending of a king and had followed the signs to the region.

"This is perfect. Maybe they can help us decide which of these two we should be focusing on." And with that, he whispered to the three that seemed to be in charge of the caravan. "You cannot enter Judea in search of a king, without acknowledging the current ruler. He will see it as insurrection. You must go to him and tell him why you are here." The men thought that the words of Satan made sense and they presented themselves to Herod.

When Herod heard that they were there in search of a newborn king he became troubled. Satan took advantage of his discomfort and whispered, "You serve at the pleasure of the Romans. Surely this one could not challenge you, he is just a babe. Find out what the prophets say." So Herod, called to him the Chief Priest and the scribes and asked where the promised Messiah was to be born. They told him that the Messiah was expected to be born in Bethlehem of Judea.

"Bethlehem!" Whispered Satan. "That is the city of David. "He will have legitimacy that you, as Rome's lap dog, do not have." Herod, bristled at the characterization of 'lap dog,' but knew it to be accurate. He listened to the whisperings of Satan and called the travelers to him and instructed that they should locate this new king and return with the information so that he too could pay him honor. As I listened to the urgings of Satan, I knew no good would come if they came back and prayed that they wouldn't.

In any event they left in the morning and for some reason we were not able to follow them. Whether it was in answer to my prayer or not I do not know, but they did not return to Herod. So Satan whispered to him, "They did not keep their promise to return to you. Maybe they intend to ally with this new king. You cannot wait until he is old enough to declare himself king. By then he will have marshalled his support."

"What would you have me do?" Asked Herod, not knowing to whom he was talking.

"The only way you can be certain to rid yourself of this upstart is to kill all the male children born in that region."

At the time, I recalled a similar order given by Pharaoh when the People of Israel dwelt in Goshen.

"That would devastate the region and cause a wailing that could not be consoled." Said Herod. Yet despite this concern, Herod listened to the whisperings of Satan and ordered the slaughter of all male infants two years of age and younger in the region. When the slaughter had been carried out we no longer could locate the boy or his family. Satan returned to Hell once again confident that he had thwarted the Lord's plans.

Confident that he had eliminated one of his threats Satan kept his attention on John. We watched as the boy named John continued to grow. He kept the Nazarite tradition as instructed by the angel Gabriel. He retreated to the desert. Satan did not bothered him there. "What harm can he do alone in the desert?" He had asked at the time.

When he returned he was a grown man. He was by all accounts a sight to see, wearing a camel hair cloak, but he spoke with authority and many people came to hear him. He encouraged the People to turn away from their sins and to be baptized as a sign of their repentance.

"He has at last sent the People a new prophet." Satan had said.

In time, to Satan's and my surprise, we eventually learned that the boy born to Mary had resurfaced. I later learned that Joseph had received a warning in a dream to take his family to Egypt. Upon their return they had settled in a small town called Nazareth.

Because Satan had not resolved his doubt regarding the boy, I was tasked with keeping watch over him. Once when the boy, Jesus was about twelve he went with his parents to Jerusalem for the feast of Passover, as they always did. Satan saw an opportunity there. "Look, here is a chance to rid ourselves of this troublesome lad so we can concentrate on John."

"What do you suggest?" I asked fearfully.

"Look, he is too old to be comfortable with the women and the children yet too young to be accepted among the men. Maybe we can isolate him and he will fall prey to those who would take advantage of his isolation."

And sure enough when the time came to return to their home he did not travel with the men as his mother thought, nor the women and children, as his father thought. Satan would have taken credit for it, except that he too lost the boy.

"Where could he be?" Asked Satan.

I continued to watch the caravan while Satan looked throughout Jerusalem to find the boy. After the first day's journey his mother and father met up, each surprised that the boy was not with the other. By the time they had inquired of their friends and relatives it was too late to return to Jerusalem. They joined a caravan returning to Jerusalem in the morning. They returned to Jerusalem the next day and searched for him until dark. As night fell, Joseph pulled the woman to him and tried to console her.

"He's not a typical boy – you know that!" He started. "All that has happened until now should convince you of that. Will not the God who hurried us off to Egypt in order to protect him do so now? Tomorrow we will go to the temple, offer sacrifice, and pray. We will find him."

"Answer me O God of Justice; from anguish release me; have mercy and hear me." Sobbed Mary, as she drew close to Joseph.

Satan returned from his searching and scoffed as he listened to the couple. "I have sent some of my angels to continue the search, but he's been alone two days and two nights, without money for bread. If they do not find him soon, he cannot last much longer alone." He said with a gleam in his eye.

The next morning Mary and Joseph fought their way through the marketplace crowded with shoppers on their way to the temple. As they entered the temple they saw a cluster of men. Some looked as if they had been there all night. As the men began to notice Mary and Joseph's presence, the throng seemed to open up and from their midst came the boy Jesus. His mother rushed to him, forgetting all social norms of propriety and proper temple decorum. She grabbed him into her arms and hugged him. Just for a moment though. Then she held him at arm's length and said to him, "Why have you done this? Your father and I have been terribly worried."

The men looked to her and apologized. "We are sorry you have suffered. He has been here since the festival. No harm has come to him. He is such an insightful boy. Where did he gain this knowledge?"

Before she could answer, Jesus spoke addressing his mother. "Why were you worried looking for me? Did you not know I would be in my Father's house, attending to his business?" As he said this, he looked to Joseph and smiled. Joseph acknowledged his smile with a slight nod and a smile of his own.

"He is consumed with zeal for his Father's house." I thought.

Satan was troubled. He had convinced himself that John was the one the Lord had wagered on, but he couldn't ignore Jesus who by now had also grown to a young man. "He's just a carpenter." Satan muttered. "What could he expect from someone so lowly?" In order to remove the doubt he had concerning John, he whispered to some of the religious leaders of the People to inquire whether John was the promised one.

In response to their questioning, John answered, "There is one coming after me whose sandal I am unworthy to loosen."

"Well that answers it I guess!" I said.

"It would seem." Answered Satan, "but we must be sure." So we continued to watch both of them.

THE VOICE AND THE WORD

t one point, to our surprise the two men we were watching met. It reminded me of our surprise when we saw their mothers meet. Jesus approached the crowd which had gathered around John. John wore the same rough cloak made of camel hair that he had when he first returned from the desert. Around his waist he wore a thick leather belt. At one time Satan had thought that he was one of whom the King had spoken. But by John's own words Satan had started to change his mind.

As Jesus approached John cried out, "Behold the Lamb of God, who takes away the sin of the world."

"Hello cousin!" Jesus said as they embraced.

"I didn't know!" John said sheepishly, thinking of all the childish things that he, as the "older" cousin, had done.

Jesus pulled from their embrace and asked to be baptized, but John resisted. "I need to be baptized by you and yet you are coming to me?"

"Allow it now, for this is fitting for us to fulfill all righteousness."

"Righteousness? Hah!" Satan spat. "I've seen enough." And with that he was gone.

Since he left, he did not see something like a dove descend onto Jesus as he came from the water. Nor did he hear the voice from Heaven say, "This is my Beloved Son, with whom I am well pleased." I recognized the voice as from the One who sat upon the throne. The One whom I served, but I did not understand what was meant by the phrase "Beloved Son." I watched as Jesus left John and those he had come with behind and wandered into the desert. I returned to Hell and informed Satan of this, certain that he would want to know.

"I don't understand! This John claims he is not the one, but the only other suspect submitted to him and was baptized." Satan started. "And now you tell me that the voice of God came out and spoke of the one named Jesus. What did the People do?"

"It is not clear whether the majority of the People actually heard the words. Some acted like it was just thunder. But clearly, both John and Jesus heard the words, and some of their followers. After the voice had spoken, Jesus went alone into the desert."

"He is mimicking his older cousin! Surely, he can't be the one." Satan exclaim, not able to hide the doubt he was feeling.

"He has entered the desert maybe there will be an opportunity to know for certain there." I offered. "Besides when John returned from the desert he began to turn the People back to God. Maybe he shouldn't be left alone."

THE FIRST CONFRONTATION

*o Satan and I watched as he spent his time in the desert. To say that he fasted would be an understatement, for the entire time he spent there he ate nothing. After some time, when he appeared to be most vulnerable Satan approached him.

"If you are the Son of God, command this stone to turn to bread."

The young man replied, "It is written, 'one does not live by bread alone, but by the very word of God.'"

"What is that nonsense?" Satan asked.

"I think he is quoting Moses." I suggested.

"I too can quote the ancients." Satan said.

Throughout this I heard, or rather I thought I heard (for sometimes angels can know a person's thoughts and it is often difficult to distinguish thoughts and speech) him cry out, "The Enemy pursues my soul!" And then quieter, "How long, Lord will you suffer the enemy to revile you. Arise and defend your cause."

Satan apparently did not hear this, because instead, he placed his hand on the man and in an instant we were whisked away and stood atop the parapet of the temple. Satan said to him, "If you are the Son of God, throw yourself down for it is written 'He will command his angels to concern themselves with you and they will uphold you lest you stumble.'"

"Quite a stumble!" I thought, but said, "Good one sir."

The young man, weakened by hunger, tottered on the heights, but said, "It is also written. 'You shall not put the Lord, your God, to the test.'"

Finally, Satan took the man to a high mountain. In an instant, all the kingdoms of the earth, both those that existed and those that were to come, flashed before Jesus' eyes. As they passed, Satan said, "All these have been given to me, and I will in turn give them to you if you will bow down before me."

For some reason I recalled, Satan's efforts to get the boy David to strike down Saul. *It was the Lord's intention to make David king (He had already had Samuel anoint him.) Had David struck Saul to take the kingship before the Lord's intended plan, he no doubt would have lost the kinship.* At the time, I didn't recognize the connection because at that moment Jesus turned and looked straight at Satan and said, what sounded like a command "Get away, Satan! It is written 'The Lord, your God, shall you worship and him alone shall you serve.'"

With that we left and Jesus found himself back in the desert. Satan did not notice that the Lord sent angels to minister to him.

Satan was determined to find out if Jesus was the one that God had predicted that he and all of Heaven would bow before. So Satan commanded some of the other fallen angels to approach him and challenge him. There was the one they called Legion, because he could manifest himself in many forms. He had possessed a man who would roam among the tombs. Legion would cause the man to cut himself and cry out without purpose or meaning. The man's family had tried everything to restrain him even resorting to chains, but the man was able to break free.

As Jesus approached Legion, speaking through the man's voice, said "What have you to do with me. Jesus, Son of the Most High God."

Jesus did not answer. He simply commanded, "Come out of the man!"

"What? – What was that that Legion called him?" Satan asked.

I didn't respond, my attention was on the interaction between Legion and Jesus. Jesus kept his focus on Legion. Whether it was the power of his voice or the command in his eyes, I do not know. But Legion was completely undone.

"I adjure you by God do not torment me." Legion pleaded.

Jesus had mercy on the demon and allowed Legion to enter a herd of pigs. We watched as the herd of pigs hurled themselves into the surf and drown. The entire event caused quite a commotion. Satan sought to capitalize on the turmoil, remarked that he would have to commend Legion when he saw him next.

The townspeople saw that the boy had been cured. But Satan whispered to them, "Anyone that can control demons like that must be one himself." They listened to the whisperings and begged Jesus to leave.

I had a different thought, remembering the chasm in Hell that so many of the angels had cast themselves into. But whatever the case, I never saw Legion again.

The incident with Legion raised the old doubts in Satan's mind. Despite John's denial that he was the one and his testament to Jesus, Satan had not been fully convinced. "What if he lies?" He resolved to settle his mind on the fact that it was either John the Baptizer or the man Jesus.

"It must be one of these, he muttered to himself. This John, is calling the People to repentance. That sounds like one of the old prophets. It has been five hundred years since he has sent a prophet. Why now? He must be something more than a prophet. But then there is this man Jesus. He is making quite a stir, he is healing the People. And rather than calling People to repentance, he has the audacity to tell them that their sins have been forgiven." Finally, he exclaimed, "I'll destroy them both!"

"Remember your stipulation to limit your efforts to those dealing with the wager?" I cautioned hopefully.

"He knows all," Satan mocked. "Surely he knew I would not honor that pledge."

"But what if he decides that your violation cancels the wager? It is not for nothing that you have been engaged in this battle all this time. You want to be elevated."

"Of course, of course! If he has not revealed to me which of these two is the one, I am within my right to attack both of them."

So in the end, he whispered into the ear of Herod Antipas, who was the son of the King that had caused the slaughter of the infants. Antipas had begun to sleep with Herodias, his cousin's wife, and the Baptizer had publicly admonished him. "You are the Tetrarch of the region. Who is this John to tell you who you can and cannot have?" It was the same enticement he had used on David.

For fear that John's condemnation would lead to an uprising, Antipas had him arrested. Satan tried to get him to have John killed, but Antipas would not. He was intrigued by his preaching, even if he did not heed it. Besides he feared the People. When Satan couldn't get him to act, he settled on another plan. Once when Antipas was giving a banquet, Herodias' daughter came and danced for the guests. The King, obviously delighted that she had please his guests offered to give her anything she asked for. Satan whispered to the young girl, "This is a once in a lifetime offer. Ask your mother what to request." To the mother he whispered, "This John has criticized your relationship with Antipas. He may not say the words but he clearly means that you are an adulterer. Be rid of him and no one will challenge your relationship. Have your daughter ask for his head. It is better that she be the daughter of the queen than the daughter of a harlot." So that's what she did. The daughter in turn ask that Antipas give her the head of the Baptizer on a platter, which he reluctantly did.

"One down, one to go!" Satan gloated as we returned to the throne room. "He is the one of whom you spoke." Satan boasted.

"You say so." The One on the throne replied.

"Why are you being so coy? If he were not the one, would you have permit me to kill the Baptizer?" Satan asked.

"That surely is not what you came here to ask." Responded the King. "You wish to know what it is that makes him special." He continued, not waiting for Satan to answer.

"Yeah." Satan answered, noticeably shaken by the Lord's preemptive statement. "What is so special about this one?"

"That you will have to see for yourself." The King said with a smile. "But that is not really your question either. You wish to know how you can win the wager."

"So tell me! What are you counting on from him?"

"I have already told you once." He said. "He will serve Me perfectly. So far He has done My Will perfectly. You remember our wager?"

"Yes I remember – but I will not be tricked as I was with Job. I must be allowed freedom to challenge him, even to death."

"Certainly God would not allow such a request!" I thought, so it shocked me to hear the Lord say with evident sadness, "He is a man, and his

tormentors must be from men. But if that torment should lead to death I will allow it. Now be gone."

Returning to Hell Satan pondered, "Now this Jesus is a different matter." Satan grumbled. "The Baptizer was easy. He was boisterous. He was not afraid to speak harshly about a person's sins. Jesus, is gentler."

"A bruised reed he will not break." I thought.

"With John, the People came for the spectacle, but with Jesus, they actually love him." Satan continued. "If he is to be stopped, we must get both the religious leaders and the politicians to act. Otherwise, one will be afraid to act less the other accuse it of ignoring the Messiah." So Satan looked for opportunities to stir up the scribes and Pharisees, as well as, the Herodians, which were the puppet rulers allowed to exist under Roman authority.

Satan whispered to the Pharisees, "This man is undermining your authority."

"But we cannot act alone against him." They answered.

"You are well versed in the Law," Satan flattered. "Surely there must be some intricacy that no matter how he answers he will either counsel violating the law given by Moses, or the law imposed by the Romans."

After pondering his suggestion amongst themselves, the Pharisees sent their disciples with some of the Herodians. One of them asked, "Teacher, we know that you are a truthful man and that you teach the way of God in accordance with the truth. And you are not concerned with anyone's opinion, for you do not regard a person's status. Tell us, then, what is your opinion: Is it lawful to pay the census tax to Caesar or not?"

But Jesus, recognized their ploy and asked, "Why are you testing me, you hypocrites?" In exasperation he said, "Show me the coin that pays the census tax." When they handed him the Roman coin. He said to them, "Whose image is this and whose inscription?"

"Caesar's."

At the question a thought occurred to me from nowhere, *"God created them in his own image."*

"Then repay to Caesar what belongs to Caesar and to God what belongs to God."

"His image is imprinted on them, they belong to him!"

Roused from these thoughts, I noticed that the delegation left him, but they continued to look for ways to trap him.

Jesus, for his part, tried to help the Pharisees understand. Once when he was approached by a man with a withered hand looking for a cure on the Sabbath, Jesus called the man to the front of the synagogue. The Pharisees were hoping he would cure the man, so they could accuse him of violating the Sabbath. Jesus, hoping to help the Pharisees understand the prophet's exhortation that God desires mercy rather than sacrifice, turned to the Pharisees and, knowing that the answer was affirmative, asked them, "Is it lawful to do good, rather than evil on the Sabbath – to save a life, rather than take it?"

Satan whispered to them, "Who is this carpenter to quiz you on the law? Do not validate his question! If you answer it, you will show that he is the teacher and you the students."

The Pharisees listened to the whisperings of Satan and did not answer.

Angered, by their refusal to answer, and grieved by their hardness of heart, Jesus cured the man despite their opposition.

Satan continued to try and undermine the ministry of Jesus in many ways. He whispered to the scribes and the Pharisees. "You know the law better than anyone. Where is this man's training? You alone know what it takes to be holy. What has this man to tell you? He undercuts your prestige – he even calls you hypocrites."

To the ruling class he whispered, "You have a good thing going here. The Romans protect your position and give you no problems. He upsets the People. You know the Romans will not tolerate another rebellion."

While many of the Pharisees paid heed to Satan's whispering, there was one named Nicodemus who was confused by what he had heard about this man. He decided that he would no longer rely on hearsay but would approach the man directly. Satan, aware of his intentions whispered to him, "You cannot risk being seen with him. Your presence will be seen as a validation. If it turns out to be false, which it surely must be, think of the scandal. Your fellow Pharisees will think you are one of his followers. You must not go!"

Nicodemus listened to Satan but he could not put aside his belief that the man must be from God. In the end he compromised and sought out Jesus at night when the crowds had gone and there was little chance that his fellow Pharisees would notice.

Satan did not stay long. He had no use for the conversation as the two men discussed what it meant to be born again or from above. I lingered longer, just long enough to hear Jesus claim to have come from above.

Later, this man who was so fearful of being seen in Jesus' presence, actually stood and defended him in front of the Pharisees. Likewise, he was not afraid to acknowledge his association with the man, even after he had been put to death. There must have been something about that encounter that Satan and I missed.

Once, as Satan was trying to discover a means to undo him, we watched and listened to Jesus speaking to his followers. Satan had already disposed of John the Baptizer and hoped that in his discussions Jesus might provide a hint of what was expected of him by the Almighty.

"Who do the People say that the Son of Man is?"

"Son of Man?" Satan asked. "Where have I heard it before?"

"The prophet Daniel." I answered. "He reported a vision involving the 'Son of Man.' his prophecy was 'one like the son of man would reach the Ancient of Days and was present before him, he received dominion, splendor, and kingship; all nations, people, and tongues will serve him. His dominion is an everlasting dominion that shall not pass away, his kingship, one that shall not be destroyed.'"

"He is claiming this title for himself! This is indeed the One of whom the Lord spoke. What was it that the Lord bet?"

"There were three Sir. The first was that one would supplant you as most favored."

"But he said that would be a woman!" Satan interrupted.

"Second," I continued. "All Flesh will be offered the opportunity to become his sons and daughters. And third, the entire heavenly host will bow down to worship one of them."

We continued to listen as his followers reported the rumors that had spread about him. But then he asked the question differently. "But who do you say that I am?" It seemed to me at the time that the first question was more theological, asking what the People remembered of the writings. This second question seemed more personal.

As I pondered this one of his disciples, Simon by name, burst out. "You are the Messiah, the Son of the living God." Jesus replied, "Blessed are you Simon, son of Jonah. For flesh and blood has not revealed this to you, but my heavenly Father ---"

"I knew!" it Satan exclaimed.

"And so I say to you," Jesus continued. "You are Peter, and upon this rock I will build my Church." He turned to our direction and continued, "And the Gates of Hell will not prevail against it."

"We'll see about that, won't we?" Satan sneered.

"Whatever you bind on earth," Jesus continued, looking our way almost as if he could see us. "Shall be bound in Heaven; and whatever you loose on earth shall be loosed in Heaven."

Next I saw Satan approach Jesus. I had seen these two verbally spar once before. At the time Satan only suspected that he was the one of whom God had spoken. He was a descendant of David, but not part of a well-regarded lineage. Nevertheless, Satan had kept his eye on him even before he was born. At the time of this last sparring Jesus had spent a long time in the desert. Although time has no meaning for angels, it was recorded as 40 days. But this time it was different. Then it had been just him and Satan. But now it seemed that Jesus was engaged in two separate conversations, it was as if he was split between two worlds.

Satan said to him, "So you are the Chosen One of God?"

"It is you that says it!" Jesus replied to Satan – to his followers he said, "We must make our way to Jerusalem."

"You cannot win!" Satan taunted. "I will not bow to you."

"You, who has known the Counsel of God, must know deep down that your time is short. Jesus said to Satan – to his followers he said, "In Jerusalem I will suffer greatly at the hands of the elders, the Chief Priests and Scribes."

"He sounds so resigned to his fate." Said Satan, directing his remark to me. "What do we know about the one to whom we are supposed to bow before?"

"He will do the Will of the Lord perfectly." I answered.

"Then we must dissuade him from continuing his course."

"I offered you the kingdoms of the earth once before. Do you go to Jerusalem, the City of the King, to claim this now for yourself?" Satan said to Jesus. To the one called Simon, he whispered, "Surely you cannot let this teacher of yours go to Jerusalem. That is where they killed the prophets."

Jesus answered Satan saying, "I go to do the Will of my Father who is in Heaven."

Peter, apparently giving heed to Satan's whisperings, responded to Jesus, "God forbid Lord! No such thing shall ever happen to you."

Jesus turned towards Peter, but looked squarely at us with fire in his eyes and said, "Get behind me Satan!" At that Satan fled. He did not see Jesus turn to Peter with a more sorrowful look, "You are judging by man's standards, and not by God's."

I had been made to watch so I sat amid the flames that were as night compared to the Light which I served. Being spirit I could feel no physical warmth though I could see it radiate from the midst of the inferno. I watched as Satan paced, "He is just a man!" He decried.

"But he is strong Sir." I responded cautiously. Seeing Satan's scowl I hurriedly continued. "Certainly you have not so quickly forgotten your efforts in the desert."

"Of course not. He could not be turned aside by concerns for his physical needs, nor baited to put God to the test. He even threw away the opportunity for untold fame and fortune if he would just pay me homage."

"A most unusual case." I said.

"No – he reminds me of another – A nazarite they called him. What was his name?"

ANOTHER HINT

"*S*amson." I answered. "He had been a Judge of the Israelites before the time of kings. He had been betrayed to the Philistines through the wiles of a woman." I said, as I recalled our interaction with him.

In those days Satan had stirred up considerable political intrigue and as a result, the Israelites were being oppressed by the Philistines. We saw an angel of the Lord approach a woman married to a Danite named Manoah. "Let us see what is to happen." I had said.

The angel said to her, "The Lord has heard you cry, and although you have been barren you will conceive and bear a son. Be careful and drink no wine or strong drink nor eat anything unclean for your son shall be a Nazarite dedicated to the Lord, even from the womb. And once he is born, take care that no razor come upon his head."

The woman said nothing but rose and told the news to her husband. Upon hearing her story her husband prayed to the Lord: "O Lord, please let the man of God whom you sent come again to us and teach us what we are to do with the child who will be born."

We did not stay to see what happened for Satan had apparently heard enough. We returned to Hell where I watched Satan muse over all that we had seen. At the time, Satan had thought that this was to be the one of whom the Lord had wagered on. He said, "Maybe this is the one. For the angel asked that he be dedicated to the Lord from the womb. What is a nazarite anyway?"

So we kept watch on this family and were there when the woman gave birth and stayed close as the boy grew. Despite Satan's efforts the boy remained faithful and grew into a man. We could tell that the spirit of the Lord was upon him.

At that time we appeared before the Lord and Satan had asked whether this was the one.

"What makes you say that?" Asked the Lord, somewhat playfully I had thought.

"It's simple, you asked that he be dedicated."

"The nazarite dedication is open to all."

"But I remember the woman, Sarah was her name. She too was barren in her old age – yet she conceived and bore a son who became the father of this People. So too her son's wife Rebekah, she was barren yet bore two sons. You seem to like to intervene in the conception process."

"It is not so much intervention," corrected the King. "I am intimately involved with that moment of conception. It is at that point when the soul attaches. It is the soul that gives life and none of them would conceive without my hand. But whether he is the one of whom I spoke, I will not say."

"Whether he is the One or not, I do not know." I had whispered to Satan. "But he is to deliver his People from the hands of the Philistine." How I came to know it and why I said it, I did not know. But at the time I knew it to be true. Satan turned to me and smiled and motioned for us to leave.

"I am certain this is the one! It is God's intention that he will free his People from oppression. But how can we get to him? He has remained faithful in his nazarite calling."

"A woman!" I had said, regretting it the moment it was spoken. Despite my regret I felt peace about the suggestion.

In time Satan sought, not once but twice, to ensnare him with his love of a woman. The last time occurred in the twentieth year that Samson served as judge. He fell in love with a woman from the valley of Sork whose name was Delilah. As he had done earlier, Satan whispered to her and she conspired with the leaders of the Philistines to find the source of his strength.

After many attempts he confided in her saying, "Since before I was born, I was dedicated to the Lord. As evidence of my dedication I have not allowed a razor to come upon my head. For it is written in our law that a nazarite must not cut his hair. If my hair should be cut I would lose the special relationship I have with the Lord."

Delilah went and told what he had shared with her and assured the leaders that she knew he had told her the truth because she could tell that he had shared his heart.

Later she caused Samson to sleep with his head in her lap. While he slept she called a man who cut his hair and bound him. When the man had finished she woke Samson and started to taunt him because she had taken the source of his strength. Satan joined in the taunting. "You have broken free in the past but where is your God now that you have cut your hair and lost the spirit of the Lord?"

Samson noticed the binding and boasted that he could break free of the bonds as he had done before. Despite his boast, he was unable to do so. Seeing that he was unable to break free, the Philistines grabbed him and led him away. They tortured him, gouging out his eyes and took him down to Gaza; bound him with metal shackles attached to a mill stone; and forced him to grind their meal.

At the time Satan had been pleased with himself for having brought down Samson. He turned to me and said, "Clearly he could not be the one. He is too prone to fall for a woman. But he will no longer judge his People, nor will he deliver them from the Philistines." To the Philistines he whispered, "Bring him out before all your people. Let them see that the gods of the Philistines are greater than the God of this man."

The Philistines offered sacrifices to their god, Dagon and made merry singing, "Our god has given Samson our enemy into our hands. The ravager of our country, who has killed so many now grinds our grain." As I watched I thought they were offering sacrifices and singing in vain. There is no God but the Lord. But then I realized that Satan was encouraging them to sing to him. "Bring him to us that we may be entertained." They shouted.

Samson was brought out to the home of one the Philistine lords. He groped as he moved and asked the men bringing him out to allow him to place his hands on the pillars so that he could gain his balance. They bound him between two pillars as all the Philistine Lords, together with 3000 men and women, watched and made sport of him.

This time, unlike when he first realized that his hair had been cut, he cried out to the Lord. "O Lord God, please remember me and strengthen me that I may be avenged on the Philistines and that they may know that you are God." With that prayer, still on his lips he pushed against the central pillars of the house – one with his right hand and the other with his left. The Lord filled him with strength and the pillars tumbled and the house collapsed, killing all those in attendance.

On seeing this Satan flew into a rage. "This man has killed more in his death, than he did while he was alive. He has delivered the Israelites more by his death than by his life."

I thought to myself, "Let destruction come upon them, let the net they hid ensnare them; let them fall to their own destruction." I said, "It seems that way sir."

Why those thoughts of some long ago judge remain with me, I didn't understand. Only later did I realize how true Satan's comment had been. As I finished my recollection, I said to Satan, "He was a Judge of this People before they had a king. Twice you tricked him through a woman, with the last time ending in his destruction."

"A woman – that's it!" Satan exclaimed, apparently forgetting that Samson's weakness had ultimately caused the destruction of the very Philistines which Satan had hoped would destroy the Israelites. "That's how we get to Jesus."

"Certainly he has shown he is in control of His passions. You will not entice him as you did with Samson." I cautioned.

"That is true, but still it will be a woman. I am sure of it. Besides, he need not succumb to her seductions – only that he be disgraced." So Satan looked for an opportunity to tempt him with a woman. The opportunity arose one night when he was dining with a Pharisee. "We'll see that he is seduced in public." Satan had said. "He will not be able to deny it."

So he induced a prostitute to go to him. "Take with you some oil," he whispered. "So that your time with him will linger."

When she walked into the house there were several men also there which she obviously did not expect. But she was not afraid of them, her trade had equipped her to interact with the powerful. Many of those in attendance had in fact tried her wares before. Some men looked down, ashamed to be reminded of their sin by her presence. Others looked at her greedily. Although her face did not betray it, I somehow knew that she loathed those looks even after all this time. They made her feel like merchandise – even though she realized that she offered herself for sale.

She walked up to him, yet I noticed some hesitation. He did not look at her as the others did. She paused before him. Her demeanor and body language had changed. No longer was she so sure of herself – gone was her seductive stance.

"What is happening?" Satan wondered out loud.

We watched as she stepped behind him, his eyes closely following her movement.

"She is stepping behind to massage his shoulders." I guessed – not knowing myself but sensing a change in the dynamic. It was then that I noticed her tears. She continued around him and now again stood directly in front of him. She knelt down and began to cry in earnest. She could no longer keep her eyes on him. As she bowed down her tears began to pour out upon his feet. She cast about looking for a towel that would normally have been used to dry a guest's feet but saw none. So she began to dry them with her hair. When she had finished she poured the oil which she had brought onto his feet and gently anointed them.

We did not stay to see what happened afterwards. "Come!" Satan demanded. "What just happened?" Satan asked when we had reached Hell.

"I couldn't tell you." I said honestly – For I could not tell Satan that the woman had been undone by his look of compassion. For Satan, despite all that he had been given, would not have been able to understand the concept.

Satan was continually frustrated in his efforts to disrupt Jesus from following the Will of God, as Satan understood it. Neither the Herodians nor the Pharisees were able to find credible grounds to have him arrested.

"Maybe we are going about this all wrong." Satan finally admitted.

"What do you mean?"

"Watch!" Was all he said as we appeared instantly in the presence of the Sanhedrin.

From the discussion, it was apparent that they too were troubled by their inability to rid themselves of the man. They were especially troubled by the rumors that he had recently brought back to life a man that had been dead and in the tomb for four days.

"This is not the first time it has been rumored that he has raised someone from the dead. Why the commotion now?" One of the men asked.

Satan whispered, "The earlier ones had happened soon after the person was thought dead. People could easily believe that the person was not really dead. But this time the man was clearly dead and in the tomb FOUR days. As word gets out all will come to believe him. You must kill this man and the one he brought from the tomb. There must not be any proof, then the rumors will die down."

One of the Pharisees said, "If we leave him alone, all will come to believe in him and the Romans will come and destroy us."

Satan whispered to the one who appeared to be in charge, Caiaphas was his name, "You are the leader, take that authority and make a bold decision. You will be remembered forever. Your colleagues are timid. What is one life to save the entire nation?"

Caiaphas listened to Satan and said, "You know nothing. Nor do you consider that it is better for you that one man should die instead of the People, so that the whole nation may not perish."

Emboldened by Caiaphas' words they decided that Jesus must be killed, and they considered amongst themselves how best to do it.

THE BETRAYAL

We returned to Hell and Satan pondered how he might deliver Jesus into their hands. "You are the watcher! There must be a way." Satan screamed.

"It won't be easy!" I started. "Remember that time he was in his hometown. You had worked on the People there telling them, 'isn't he the carpenter, Mary's son?' They chased him out of town all the way to a cliff, if you would remember. But they were unable to do as you had urged. In fact he walked through the crowd and they were unable to touch him." I paused, hoping he would give up the plan, when he didn't capitulate, I continued. "He has grown such a following. When He's out and about there is always a crowd. The leaders won't risk taking him in front of a crowd."

"Don't tell me how it won't work." Satan remarked sarcastically. "Tell me what will!"

"Well," I paused, unsure whether I should continue. "He frequently goes away to pray. If they knew when and where, he could be taken then." Even as I spoke these words, a part of me felt I was betraying my Lord. Yet a calm came over me, which brought peace of mind as I continued.

"And how do we do that?" Satan asked, showing his frustration at being reminded of his earlier failure.

"He has surrounded himself with a group of men. Maybe one of them can be convinced to provide the religious leaders the information."

"Which one?"

"Do you recall the time when you sought to seduce him while he dined with the Pharisee?"

"Why do you bring up these failures?" He bellowed.

"One of his followers," I continued, enjoying his discomfort at being reminded of his earlier defeat. "Judas, was his name. He complained about the oil being wasted when she anointed his feet. He was rebuked by Jesus. At the time, his face showed hurt and confusion as he clearly thought care for the poor was an important part of what the 'Anointed One' was to do. He is clearly focused on the political element of the prophecies. Maybe he is the one you should use!"

Satan took my advice and approached Judas shortly thereafter. "You know this man you follow has alienated both the religious leaders and the Herodians." It sounded more like a question. "They would pay handsomely for information how to arrest him without a lot of people around." Judas did not respond, but I saw his hand move toward the money bag that he carried. He shook his head and we left.

As we returned to Hell I was relieved that Satan had failed to convince Judas to betray Jesus. But Satan did not appear concerned. "Money may be his weakness, but he won't turn Jesus over for money alone. This Flesh is a complicated animal, many conflicting thoughts and motives. He has invested too much of himself in following him these past three years. I will use that to our advantage."

It was not long after that when we were there as they walked through the countryside. Satan approached him, "Why do Peter, James, and John always get to walk nearest to him? Do you remember when James and John had the boldness to ask to be seated at his right and left when he established his kingdom?" Judas didn't respond, but it was clear that Satan had struck a nerve. We left as Satan wanted the seed he had planted to germinate.

A few days later he again approached Judas. "I know how you can become the favorite." Again he did not respond, but Satan continued. "Remember on the road when he had declared Peter the rock? He rebuked Peter when Peter tried to dissuade him from going to Jerusalem. He wants to have his confrontation with the Temple Leaders."

Again Judas did not respond but he appeared to be contemplating Satan's words.

It was not long when it seemed that Satan's words were prophetic. He, along with those who followed him entered Jerusalem. Although he normally walked, on this occasion he had sent some of his disciples ahead to procure a donkey for him to ride.

As he entered the city, the People began to cry out, "Hosanna in the Highest." And throw palm branches in his path.

"This will not do!" Satan bellowed. "They will not be able to put him to death if he has the backing of the People."

Satan whispered to a nearby soldier. "Do you not hear what they are saying? Surely they are challenging the authority of Rome. You know this People. They look for a deliverer. If it becomes known that you were aware of this usurper and did nothing, it will mean your life."

Satan's words had the desired impact and he ran to the praetorian to advise his commander.

"Sir, the People are announcing the coming of a king!" Exclaimed the young soldier, out of breath from running.

What do you mean?" Asked the commander. "Calm down and speak!"

After catching his breath, the soldier continued. "I was on patrol near the city gate when the People began to gather. You know this People are troublesome so I drew closer. They are distrustful of us but I overheard them whispering. They spoke of a prophesied One who was to come. He is here now! They were yelling for him and throwing their coats and palm branches before him."

"How many men accompany him?" Asked the commander, always the practical man. He turned and saw Jesus riding through the streets on the back of a donkey.

"Twelve sir, and – and some women." Replied the soldier, realizing only now that the Man was not a threat.

"It would seem right that this People's king would arrive on an ass." The commander smirked. "But I think Caesar need not fear this threat." He said, as his smirk turned to a grin. "Now back to your post."

Shortly after this Jesus entered the temple district and caused quite a commotion. He overturned tables and set free the animals the merchants had brought to sell for sacrifices. People approached him and sought healing and the children danced around him singing "hosanna to the son of David." He enraged the religious leaders, the teachers, as well as the ruling class. Satan whispered to Judas, "This is your chance.

Did you not join him thinking him to be the Messiah? Listen to the children, they know what the rulers do not. The way forward is clear. He has come to Jerusalem and this is the final confrontation. It is in this confrontation that he will reveal himself as the Messiah. Go to them and tell them you will deliver him to them. It is what he wants, you will show yourself superior to Peter and all the others."

Although Judas never responded, he did as Satan suggested. He went to the Chief Priests and agreed to deliver Jesus into their hands.

THE BEGINNING OF THE END

*W*e watched as he was led to the whipping post. He went without hesitation, but there was a look of fear on his face. Satan whispered to him. "I remember the conditions God first placed on me regarding Job. At first he would not let me lay a hand on him. Surely what you are about to get is worse than anything I did to Job."

As he finished, the torturers began their bloody work. We watched as the whips tore the flesh from his back. As an angel, being pure spirit, I have no way of understanding the pain in the flesh. But as I watched the skin tear, the blood flow, the anguish on the man's face, and the looks given by those who witnessed the beating, I caught myself wondering if God's decision to make Flesh was worth what this man was enduring. It was almost more than I could bear. Even those who watched tried to hide their faces to shield themselves from the brutality, but were inexplicably drawn to watch as if the sound of each stripe laid across his back beckoned. But I had been made to watch, so I did.

We returned to Hell when the beating was finished. Not satisfied that he had caused an innocent man to be arrested, sentenced to death and horribly beaten, he was animated as he considered the events of the day.

"I cannot understand why I was not able to enter that upper room. What happened after I left?"

Earlier that evening we had watched the group enter a room above the house of one of his followers. Satan and I had tried to follow, but for some reason we were blocked. At the time Satan had asked how this was possible. I reminded him that a similar thing happened when we had tried to approach the young girl who would become his mother.

But tonight, shortly after the group had entered the room the man named Judas, the one who had agreed to do Satan's bidding left the room. Satan had chosen to follow him with instruction that I was to keep watch and that he would summon me if anything happened. Once Satan left, I was able to enter the room.

The night happened to be during the feast of Passover. Judas must have left sometime during the meal because when I entered they were all still around the table.

When Satan returned, confident that Judas would not back out of the betrayal, he was no longer concerned with what was happening in that room, he was satisfied with the brief synopsis that I gave him.

"I know what he intends to do? And I know how to stop it." He bragged.

"What? How?" I asked.

"You are the watcher – Do you not remember what happened with the man named Abraham and his son Isaac?"

It was Abraham that was the father (at least in the flesh) of this People. It was by watching his line that Satan had concluded that the One about whom God had spoken would be of this People. It had happened roughly 13 years after God had kept his promise to Sarah, to give her a child. The Lord had asked Abraham to sacrifice his son Isaac. As Abraham prepared to slay the boy, an angel intervened and stopped him.

"It is the same. He agreed with my stipulation that this one could be put to death, because he intends to spare him at the last minute like he did Isaac. Just as Abraham didn't know that Isaac would be spared, I'm sure this one does not know that he will be spared. All we have to do is scare him into deciding not to go through with it. If he backs down before God can save him, I win the bet."

ANOTHER CONFRONTATION

We watched as Jesus, along with his followers, left the room. They retreated to a garden as was his custom. He separated himself from the others and began to pray in earnest. From the turmoil on his face it was clear that this man actually believed that he was about to die.

"Son of Man!" Satan spat with derision in his voice. "You claim that title, linking yourself to all that is said by the prophets. Do you recall all that Isaiah said about you then? You are to be crushed for their sins. Are willing to die for the sins of the world – are you? I have certain knowledge that you might want to know." He taunted. "Do you know that millions will kill and be killed in your name? Which side are you dying for?"

"Abba Father, all things are possible to you! Take this cup away from me, but not what I will but what you will."

"How about that mothers will one day kill the child in their womb. You can't really be dying for that?"

"Father, if you are willing, take this cup away from me, still not my will but yours be done."

Satan continued with torments such as these, but the man would not back down.

"Father if it be your will, let this cup pass from me, but your will not mine."

Shortly after this Judas arrived accompanied by the temple guards and an assortment of men sent by the Chief Priests and elders. Judas embraced Jesus and greeted him with a kiss. At this sign the men moved in to arrest Jesus.

"How ironic, that one who accompanied you all this time and shared your last meal would betray you, with a sign of friendship?" Whispered Satan.

To Peter Satan whispered, "Are you going to stand there and let him be taken? You brought a sword, defend him." Whether Peter listened to Satan or merely recalled Jesus' prediction that he would deny him, I do not know, but he struck out wildly with a sword and a small skirmish ensued. Although Satan tried to foment the scuffle. "They are coming to your rescue, take the position which you have already claimed." Satan whispered to Jesus. But Jesus ignored him and quickly instructed his followers to lay down their weapons. Before it was over, however, the ear of a servant of the High Priest had been severed. Jesus healed the ear before he was bound and led away.

As they were leading him toward the temple, Satan whispered to the man who had been injured. Your master would want to know about your ear and how he healed it."

The man listened to Satan's words and led him to the High Priest Annas and told him all that had happened.

Satan whispered to Annas, "Your fellow High Priests want to kill this man. Find out if he truly is the Messiah. You know Nicodemus also inquired of him. If you recognize and acknowledge him before them, you will be greatly reward."

Annas asked him, "So tell me, how many followers do you have? What do you teach them that they would follow you?"

Satan whispered to Jesus, "Here is an advocate that can help you in the trial that will surly come. He will tell you what to say to them, that you need not fear."

But instead Jesus answered Annas saying, "I have spoken publicly in the synagogue and in the temple area. I have not spoken anything in secret. Ask those who heard me what I have said."

Satan whispered to the guard standing by. "That was no answer! How dare he speak like that to the High Priest? Make him answer!"

The guard listened to Satan and struck Jesus saying, "Is that the way you answer the High Priest?"

To Jesus Satan whispered, "They will have an answer to their questions before you are through. Answer him and save yourself the agony."

But Jesus simply said to the guard, "If I have spoken wrongly testify to the wrong; but if I have spoken rightly, why do you strike me?"

Annas, realizing that there was nothing to be gained by further questioning, ordered that he be taken before the whole Sanhedrin.

The trial before the Sanhedrin was primarily a sham. Caiaphas asked him plainly, "If you are the Messiah, tell us."

Satan whispered to Jesus, "Is that not why you came? That they would come to believe that you are what you claim to be?"

Once again Jesus appeared to be having two separate conversation, To Caiaphas Jesus said, "If I tell you, you will not believe. And if I question, you will not respond." Turning to Satan he said, "I came to do the will of my Father who is in heaven."

Satan, obviously troubled by Jesus' words, whispered to Caiaphas, "You are High Priest! Make him answer plainly."

Whether Caiaphas listened to Satan or honestly wished to be sure in his decision, I do not know, but he said, "I order you to tell us under oath before the living God whether you are the Messiah."

Jesus answered him saying, "You have said so, but I tell you," Looking in our direction he continued, "From now on you will see the Son of Man seated at the right hand of the Power and coming on the clouds of Heaven."

This last comment sent Satan into a rage. "He claims to be the 'Truth' whatever that means. Bring false testimony against him. If he values truth he will defend himself."

Satan's words rang true with the High Priests and the elders so they brought a number witness against him but their testimony was often in conflict. In the end, they relied on his earlier proclamation to support the charge of blasphemy.

"Blasphemy?" Satan asked. But then his eyes lightened. "Blasphemy is a religious charge, they have no power to sentence him to death. He will not be led to death the Lord's plan for this man will come to nothing." But Satan's optimism was short lived. His earlier efforts to have him killed were too thorough, for in the morning the Chief Priests and the elders took him to Pilate, who was the Roman proconsul in charge of the region. Knowing that the Romans would not intervene in a religious dispute, they brought political charges against him.

It was odd to hear the "father of lies" advocate for the truth as he tried to get Pilate to acquit him. But Satan was primarily interested in undermining God's Will as he understood it. Throughout the exchange Jesus would not defend himself. Twice Pilate admitted that he found no guilt in Jesus, but the High Priests and elders, were insistent. Satan reminded Pilate of his tradition to release a captive during the Passover. When Pilate offered to release Jesus according to his practice, the Jews refused. If they could not be sure he was who the People said he was, they would be rid of him. Pilate's own wife came and urged him to have nothing to do with execution of Jesus. But in the end, Pilate succumbed to the political realities and allowed Jesus to be sentenced to death, laying the political charges against him. "Jesus the Nazorean, the King of the Jews."

We watched as the soldiers led him from the courtyard. They placed on him the timber which would become the instrument of his death. We watched as he began his journey to the place of execution. As much as I despised it, I wondered at the efficiency of the Roman means of punishment. By making him, and the others, process through the village, the entire town was exposed to the cruelty, and would come to fear the Roman power. I looked to Satan and saw him beam as a father beams with pride over a son's accomplishments, and realized that he was the originator of the Roman cruelty.

It was not long before the effects of the previous night's scourging and the endless taunting to which he was subjected took its toll. He fell to the ground under the weight of the wood.

It was then that Satan spoke. "Why do you continue? Lie there and be done with it. Surely your death, here in the streets of Jerusalem, would satisfy that God of yours."

Jesus looked in our direction, but not at us. I would say he was looking through us. I saw his lips move, but could not hear what he said. I turned to see what lay behind us and saw that he had fixed his eyes on his mother. She urged him to get up with that same look she had used some three years before to ask him to help an embarrassed newlywed couple that had run out of wine.

He struggled to gain his feet, but the weight of the timber was too much for his weakened condition. Satan taunted him further. "Clearly God did not mean you to continue. He made that flesh of yours, it cannot bear to go on."

Again he moved his lips, this time I could make out what he said. "For man it is impossible, but not for God!" I recalled that he had said the same thing to his followers when they had asked "who could be saved?" It was only later that I realized the true meaning of those words.

As I took all this in, I barely noticed that Satan had been urging the Roman centurions to beat him to get up. One, who had seemed to take pleasure during the previous night's scourging heeded Satan's prompting and began to beat him ruthlessly. Another, whether due to compassion or out of Roman efficiency I do not know, moved to the crowd and grabbed a man and pressed him into service. Reluctantly Simon, for that was his name, helped Jesus get to his feet and continue the journey that would end in death.

As he began to rise, a woman pushed through the crowd. Those around her were offended at her efforts. This offense soon turned to shock as she uncovered her head and used her veil to wipe Jesus' face. This last show of compassion seemed to have an effect on him, because he rose to his feet and, with Simon's help, continued his journey towards the place of execution.

It was not long though that he fell again. Satan continued his jeering tempting him to lay down and die. As much as I loathed Satan, I had to agree with him, this Flesh could not take much more. As he lay on the ground he looked into the crowd and spoke. "Daughters of Jerusalem, do not weep for me; weep instead for yourselves and for your children, for indeed, the days are coming when people will say, 'Blessed are the barren, the wombs that never bore and the breasts that never nursed.' At that time, people will say to the mountains, 'Fall upon us!' and to the hills, 'Cover us!' for if these things are done when the wood is green what will happen when it is dry?" After saying this, he again got to his feet and left the city gates.

We could see the mount that would be the end of his torture. It seemed that as he got closer, his determination to reach the place increased. It was almost as if he desired the death that was awaiting him there. It was this desire that strengthened him as he began to walk up the slope. As he continued his struggle, I recalled the young boy named Isaac who also struggled up a slope under the burden of wood:

At that time the boy was travelling with his father and one of his father's servants. Abraham, his father, had told him that they were going to make a sacrifice to the Lord. As they arrived at the foot of the mountain, the father had told the servant to remain and that they would return after the sacrifice. The wood for the sacrifice had been placed on the boy's young shoulders while Abraham carried the fire. Midway through the ascent the boy realized that they had brought with them no lamb to offer as a sacrifice, so he asked his father about it.

"You need not worry, the Lord will provide for the sacrifice." Was all that his father had said.

He loved his father and had heard him tell of the faithfulness of God, so he let the matter rest. When they reached the summit, Abraham took the wood from the boy and built an altar. The boy looked around and still he saw no offering. Then to his amazement his father approached and began to bind him. He thought to resist but several thoughts clambered in his head. It was his father. He knew his father loved him, he had been the child of his old age. But what eventually calmed him was that he recalled what his father had told the servant. His father had said THEY would return after the sacrifice. He knew his father would not lie. So he let himself be bound and laid upon the altar. In the end, although the father showed his willingness to offer his son as a sacrifice, the Lord sent an angel to spare the boy. It was a test of the father' commitment to God. As I watched Jesus ascend the hill, I saw it as a test of the son's trust in the father.

"Did you not see your disciples flee at your arrest last night? Surely they are not worthy of what you have suffered, nor what is to follow. You said you have the power to lay down your life and take it up again. Use that power and end this."

It was not long after that he met his mother. Satan whispered to him, "You cannot leave her childless! You saved that woman from that fate by raising her son. Surely your mother deserves that as well. If you die she will have no protector."

Satan looked toward the woman and for the first time was able to approach her. He whispered, "He will listen to you, remember that time at the wedding? Ask him to spare his life to protect you." His mother, appearing not to notice Satan or his words heaved a sigh and whispered to herself, "He told me that my heart too would be pierced." And then with more conviction, looking toward Heaven she finished, "I said it once and as hurtful as it is now I'll say it again, may it be done according to your Will."

Returning to Jesus, Satan whispered. "Who is this stranger they have asked to help you? Why is there none of your followers here to help? Do you remember that day on the path, when you asked your followers who the People say you are?" Satan asked.

I did not know where this line of questioning was going. But Jesus with a knowing gaze indicated that he was aware of Satan's intentions.

"They declared you the Messiah, God's Chosen One. Chosen for what? Slaughter?"

I thought, *"Like a lamb you lead me to slaughter!"* But said nothing.

"What of the one you declared Rock?" Satan continued. "I knew you saw me then, when you said 'the gates of Hell would not prevail.' Well look where you are. You are about to die and enter into the gates of Hell from where there is no return. And did you not see the one you called Peter in the courtyard last night? I hear that he pledged his undying support that night in the upper room, yet he failed to come to your aid."

I knew Satan's last statement to be a lie. For it had been Peter who drew a sword when the soldiers appeared. Not being a warrior, he swung wildly, and struck the ear of a man. Jesus had told him to put away the sword as he healed the man's ear. Peter had looked confused that night, just as he did that time on the path when Jesus had told him that he was thinking like men.

"I guess I can understand his fear at disclosure, when he first denied you. But he denied ever knowing you TO A SLAVE GIRL. Surely he is not capable of carrying your Church (whatever that is). End this thing until you can find a more worthy leader."

Satan was relentless in his efforts to get Jesus to lay down his cross. Despite his torments, Jesus remained silent. Finally, they reached the place where the cross would be erected. Two other men were there already. As they positioned the cross, it became apparent that he would be placed between the two men.

As they raised the cross and allowed it to settle into place, I wondered aloud – not sure where the thought had come from, "Doesn't it seem that every time you set a snare for them it ends up working against you?"

"You are the watcher, you should know." He said absently as he watched the man Jesus as he struggled to breathe up on the cross. But then in a flash, Satan's face changed and he became animated. "He has tricked me. It is not like Abraham and his son. He is going to let this man die!"

"For what purpose?" I asked.

"With Isaac, it was the test of the father, Abraham. But I had it wrong! This one is not the Father, and where is the son?" He asked, more to himself. "Don't you recall that he calls himself 'the Son of God? God intends to allow this one to die, to 'do his Will perfectly' is what he said. Just to win our wager. We must not allow him to die."

"What can you do to stop it?" I asked.

To one of the men being crucified along with him, Satan whispered, "He is known for his mercy and forgiveness. Beg him to save himself and you as well." The man listened to Satan's murmurings, but the one on the other side spoke out.

"Have you no fear of God! We are under the same sentence of death, we are guilty, but this man is innocent." I can't say that he turned to Jesus, but his tone and demeanor changed and he said, "Jesus, remember me when you come into your kingdom."

Jesus, gasping for breath answered him saying, "Amen, I say to you, today you will be with me in paradise."

"Paradise? You promise what you cannot deliver. You cannot really believe that God will save you. The Sadducees are wrong. I have the power of death, and I do not give up my prize." Still the man on the cross did nothing.

Satan whispered to those watching, "Do not fear for this man, he saved other, he can save himself too. Call out to him and urge him to come down."

"Did not Solomon write of one such as this?" Asked someone from the crowd. "I remember it, 'For if the righteous one is the son of God, God will help him.'"

Satan changed his tone and to the one on the cross he whispered, "You hear them? They want to know if it is true. I remember in the desert, you would not prove for me that you were the Son of God, but for them, surely you wish for them to believe."

When Jesus did not respond, Satan continued. "You once said you have the power to lay down your life and take it up again. Show forth your power and they will believe. Did you not come to save the lost sheep of Israel? Save them by a show of power which they cannot ignore."

Satan continued his torment of the man, urging him to save himself and prove all that he had claimed. Through it all his mother remained at the foot of the cross. Satan again tried to urge him to save himself for her sake. This time, instead of responding to Satan, he called out to his mother, "Woman, here is your son!" indicating to the only one of his inner circle that had been brave enough to be there. To the disciple he said, "Here is your mother." He looked at Satan and through his anguish, I thought I saw him attempt a smile.

Shortly after that, he cried out in a loud voice, "Father, into your hands I commend my spirit," and died. At that moment I knew that Satan had lost his bet. Satan did too!

I watched as they removed his lifeless body from the Cross. His mother, Mary enfolded him in her arms weeping sorrowfully, yet somehow in peace with the death of her son. Satan watched the scene in fury.

Then my attention was drawn to the woman, his mother. She had been there at the cross watching his torment. She had been there at the end when he had declared, "It is finished!" I recalled that she had been there at the beginning too.

Once when we were roaming the area of Judea we saw the man Jesus and his mother in Cana of Galilee at a wedding. (It was the same event which Satan had mentioned only hours before.) He was joined by a number of men who had begun to travel with him. (For some reason they had been drawn to him or him to them, because as of that time he had performed no miracles.) At some point during the week-long celebration the family ran out of wine for their guests. Mary, who always seemed to be aware of other people's distress, asked the groom's father who confided in her his concern. Without another word, she approached her son and pulled him aside. "They have no wine!" She told Him. No command, no request, just an appraisal of the base facts.

"Woman, what does this have to do with me?" He asked. It sounded more like a plea than a question. His voice quavered slightly as he spoke it.

She gently placed her hand on his and looked into his eyes.

In an apparent reply he spoke. "My hour has not yet come." This time more steadily.

She looked again at him, this time nodding. I had the picture of a mother bird prodding her brood from the nest to force their first flight. She turned to the attendants and said simply, "Do whatever he tells you."

As I watched her caress the broken body of her son, I wondered if she had known this would be the end, would she have encouraged him to take that first step. But then I recalled the time in the temple, when he was just eight days old. *Satan had been frustrated because for some reason he could not get near the woman. From the moment of her birth, every time we drew near her, Michael, the guardian of the Lord was present. So Satan did not see as she entered the temple with Joseph, her husband, carrying the child. She approached an old man, the one who was to perform the ceremony, his name was Simeon.*

As Simeon took the child, his eyes widened and he exclaimed. "Now Lord you may let me your servant go in peace, for I have seen your salvation which you have prepared for the entire world to see. This boy shall be a light for the gentiles, and bring glory to your People Israel."

As I watched the man perform the ceremony, I noticed that the woman, was not paying any attention, she was obviously pondering the words that had just been spoken. Simeon must have noticed too because he looked at her and said, "This child is destined for the rise and fall of many in Israel. He will be a sign of contradiction and you yourself will be pierced by a sword."

With that warning, even as cryptic as it was, she must have had an idea. Yet she never wavered or tried to dissuade him. Even that time in Capernaum when she sought him out. She had sent someone to tell him she wanted him, but he had declared to the crowd, "My mother and my brothers are those who hear the Word of God and act on it." In her heart, she knew that had she been faithful to God her entire life, so she knew he was not speaking for her, but for the benefit of the crowd, but you could tell from her

148

face that the looks of the crowd hurt her. As I completed these thoughts it dawned on me. Satan, once being the Most Favored, had been created "to listen" is what the Lord had said. Whereas Satan revolted upon hearing the Lord's plan – this woman accepted it completely. She was now the Most Favored.

My thoughts returned to the moment and as I pondered all that I had seen, it came to me. *"All the events of Man had culminated in this moment. It all started that moment in the throne room, with the wager. Oh how he loves to wager."* I remember his wager over one of his servants Job. Satan had lost that one. But until the very end it never seemed to dawn on Satan that he would lose this one also. The Lord had been so confident, *"I guess when you are all knowing it's not much of a risk."* As that realization dawned on me we were brought to the throne room.

"Do you not see," said the Lord. "All you have done has brought them to me, just as I said. For even in your disobedience you cannot help but do my Will."

"That can't be!" Said Satan dubiously.

"Absolutely!" He started. "They were created with free will, I could not teach them evil because it is not in my nature, and by your temptations you taught them the knowledge of evil. The ones who have followed Me know that to choose evil is deadly.

"I knew your hatred for my Beloved was all consuming. My destruction with the flood, caused you to temper your attacks on them. In the same way, my faithful servant Job, suffered so that you would be restrained for not just one season but for three. Do you not realize how many his suffering protected?

"You stirred up Laban to cheat Jacob of his intended, by giving him Leah instead of Rachel. But you see Jacob was a young man and chose Rachel over Leah for the wrong reasons. It was through Leah that the line of the Savior would come. In your treachery you furthered my purpose.

"In the same way, did you not notice that the People dwelt in Goshen while they grew in number? You stirred up Pharaoh to destroy the male children just when it was time that they should leave. It was through that process that Moses was cast into the river and found by Pharaoh's daughter. Do you think that was by chance? As a result he was able to grow accustom to the ways of the court and be granted access to Pharaoh that he might plead for the release of my People.

"And your meddling in the desert, and the subsequent 40 year delay helped the People to grow to a number where they could inhabit the land that I had given them. Had they come straight from Egypt, they would have too easily joined the customs of the Canaanites as so many did anyway.

"Your political intrigue, throughout the history of this People, help to bring them back to Me each time they grew complacent.

"Even when you devised to strike the Baptist, you did my Will. He had been sent to announce the Messiah. Even though he denied the title and even pointed out my Son, many continued to follow him, rather than the true Messiah. While he lived they followed the voice, rather than the Word. His death was necessary and once again by your actions you carried out my Will.

"I thought you might recognize it when you dealt with Samson, but every time you attacked him, he killed more and more of the enemy of my People. At the time you even complained that he had saved more by his death than by his life.

"Did you not notice that with each covenant I made the circle grew? Each time you caused it to be broken, the next one encompassed more People. The first covenant with Adam and Eve was expanded to include the entire family when I made my covenant with Noah. With Abraham the covenant expanded yet again to include a nation. With David, the covenant encompasses an entire kingdom. And finally, this new covenant which you have caused to be sealed by the blood of my Son is now universal."

Satan stammered in disbelief. "That – That cannot be! Clearly, the entire world of Flesh does not know of you."

"That is true." Said the King. "But do you not remember that Jesus established a Church before his Passion? It will be the job of the Church to spread that knowledge. And thanks to you, I no longer just walk beside them as I did in the Garden, but shortly I will dwell within them and they will have power from on high to accomplish all that is required.

"And now, do you wish to meet the one to whom you and all the heavenly host must bow before?" And with that the One on the throne transformed and took the form of a man. It was the man on the cross.

"That's impossible!" Satan cried.

"But it is true!" Said the King. And I watched as the whole heavenly host continued its praises to the one seated on the throne, the refrain slightly changed. "Holy, holy, holy, is the God Creator, and Redeemer."

Satan and I returned to Hell, and we saw the One from the cross, on the opposite side of the chasm that I had once tried to leap. Satan was fearful seeing the One whom he had just seen sitting on the throne. But the resemblance of the man, must have emboldened him because he said, "What are you doing in my realm?"

"Although you have claimed it as your own, it was created through Me by the Father, and these souls which have been detained here until my coming now have a choice. And to them, He spoke:

"Once I walked upon the earth and Adam and Eve knew Me well. By their choice humankind lost the grace which enabled them to know and serve Me well. Nevertheless, I did not forsake you, My Beloved. Since that time you still had the ability to discern the reality of God. My attributes are shown forth in the beauty of creation, and the order of the seasons, for instance. Yet in your confusion, you saw these attributes of the created world and praise them rather than the Creator itself. I tell you now that all those things were created through Me and for Me.

"As a result, I allowed you to continue your futile ways until such time as I could raise up a People who could show you the truth. I gave them my law so that you could see my holiness through them. But they failed." He looked to Abraham, and those who surrounded him, and continued, "But this did not surprise me, you are incapable of being holy as I am holy. My law was meant to show you this reality, to help you realize that on your own you could not attain the holiness for which you longed." Here he looked at a group which I knew to be Pharisees.

"Under the Law I desired sacrifices so you could learn to give to me, that which you thought was yours. I say thought was yours because 'the earth is the Lord's and all that it contains.' But now you must use what you have learned. You have been created with free will and your will is really all that you can rightfully claim as your own. I set before you this day a choice, life and death, a blessing and a curse. I call Heaven and Earth today to be witness. Choose life that you might live forever in the Love of God." Not a word was spoken but I noticed that some of those present began to head for the precipice. Adam and Eve, first then Noah, Abraham and Sarah, and all the patriarchs followed.

Satan cried out, "It is a trick, there is no bottom there. You will fall for all eternity." But many continued to head for the cliff and soon an entire multitude followed and took the plunge toward what appeared to be unending plummet. But I remembered my own fall, how it had led me back to the throne room.

When all those who had heard his testimony and come to believe in God's Goodness had fallen into the abyss there was silence. And I heard one of the angels cry out, "What of us?"

You, by your nature, beheld the Father as he truly is. You have rejected he who IS and therefore, my words and the choice I presented this day are not meant for you. But you too have a choice, it is one which some of you have already taken. End your rebellion and bow before Me as vanquished foe and leap into the void. I watched as I saw some, though not many, approach the edge and bow before the Lord and leap over the edge, relieved to be done with their resistance. From the chasm I heard, "Holy, holy, holy, is the God Creator, and Redeemer."

With that we were once again in the throne room. And the Lord, no longer looking as the man, but now in all his Glory, spoke. "Do you not see that you have lost this bet? Bow before Me and end your rebellion."

"You have not won, I have angels. . ."

"They are my angels!" He interrupted.

"That have not bowed." Satan continued without acknowledging the correction.

"*The bet was that the heavenly host would bow before one of the Flesh.*" I thought. "Surely that has happened, both in Heaven and in Hell." But I said nothing.

"And besides, the throne of the one to supplant me remains empty."

"That is true." Said the One seated on the throne. "It is reserved for my Queen . . ." "My mother!" As the one on the throne, appeared once again as the one who had endured the cross. "My Church!" The one on the throne continued in that airier voice. "But just as surely as I knew this day was coming when we first made our wager, it will be accomplished. You contended with the woman and her offspring and failed, would you now contend with My church?"

"I will not bow to you. I still can bring death and destruction to those whom you love."

"Not so!" He replied, and with that we were back on earth in a garden.

Although not as lush, it reminded me of that Garden so long ago, as Flesh counts time. A woman approached a tomb. A large stone that had once covered it had been rolled aside. One of the Lord's messengers appeared to her and spoke. Although we could not hear, he had apparently spoken of the One that had been laid in the tomb, for she left there and returned shortly with two of his followers. It was then that I realized it was the tomb in which the One on the cross had been buried. The men entered the tomb, first the elder, followed shortly by the younger one. After spending just a moment there, they came out, looking perplexed.

They made ready to leave the garden, but the woman could not bear to leave the tomb of the man who had shown her such love and whom she had come to love completely. The men left the woman crying at the tomb, talking together about what it all meant.

As I have said, time is not the same for angels as for Flesh, but it must have been but a few minutes later, for she was still crying, Michael and Gabriel appeared to the woman. "Why are you crying?" They asked her.

"Because they have taken away my Lord and I do not know where."

They said nothing but indicated with their eyes. The woman and I turned in the direction that they had been looking and I saw the Lord, appearing once again as the man from the cross. She did not recognize him and asked whether he was the gardener.

"I am a gardener, you might say!" He said with a smile. I once again recalled the beautiful garden that had been created through him, who I now knew was the very Word of God.

"If you have taken him from here, tell me where he is that I might go to him."

"Maryām!"

She looked to him and, recognizing not the voice but the unmistakable love with which he spoke, saw him whom she longed for.

And with that we were once again in the throne room. "You no longer have the power of death. It has been taken from you."

The words spoken by the Lord had an impact on Satan which I had not ever seen. He was diminished. He lost the arrogance which he had shown since he had spoken rather than listen, so long ago.

EPILOGUE

"Contend with his Church!" Satan said with contempt. "You call this band that has gathered around the One a Church? Did they not abandon him on that night he was arrested? In fact, if I remember correctly, one even ran away naked, rather than be arrested with him. And did not the one he appointed leader, deny that he even knew the Man? We will destroy this band before they can establish a foothold."

With that we were back on earth. Satan returned to the teachers of the law who he had manipulated so easily against the Nazorean. This time he turned them against a man named Stephen. It had started when some converts to Judaism from Cyrene, Alexander, Cilicia, and others from the region of Asia, became jealous over the signs and wonders he was performing.

"Who is he that would debate you?" Satan whispered to some of them. "What training does he have? Have you not seen him waiting on tables, tottering on widows? If word gets out that he has bested you in a debate, who will listen to you?"

The men listened to Satan and thought that his words made sense. So they conspired to incite others to attack Stephen in an attempt to ruin his reputation. "Say to the elders and the crowd that he has spoken blasphemously."

When the elders and scribes heard the allegations they grabbed Stephen and brought him to the Sanhedrin. The men, emboldened by the success of their earlier lies said, "This man never stops saying things against the law and the temple. He is a follower of Jesus, the Nazorean, who claimed that he would destroy the temple. Jesus and this man are trying to change the law handed down by Moses."

Satan whispered to the scribes and the elders and the men of the Sanhedrin. "Oh! The Nazorean! Obviously, your beatings have not silenced his followers. You must be more drastic if you wish to stop it." A young man named Saul sat at the feet of Gamaliel who shook his head during the exchange. Saul on the other hand nodded in agreement.

We watched as a host of angels came. Satan cowered at the host, but they were not for him. Instead they formed a hedge around Stephen. The Lord had sent them to his defense. I was reminded of something Jesus had said. "When they take you before synagogues and before rulers and authorities, do not worry about how or what your defense will be or about what you are to say. For the Holy Spirit will teach you at that moment what you should say." Instantly his disposition changed. Instead of the look of fear and uncertainty which had just moments before shrouded his face, a look of calm and confidence overtook him. His whole face reflected the change. It must have been apparent to the others, because the high priest was slightly taken aback when he turned to Stephen and ask, "Is this so?"

We listened as Stephen recounted the significant events of God's plan of Salvation. Satan cringed as Stephen's words reminded him of all his failures. As Stephen continued his discourse Satan's discomfort turned to rage. "Who is this child to recount to you the history of God's work?" He bellowed. The violence of his outburst did not have the effect he had desired. He was always more effective with a whisper. He calmed himself and whispered, "He will stir up the People. He will remind them of this Jesus and that you had him killed. You will lose their trust. The Romans will not tolerate another rebellion."

As Stephen spoke, the elders, scribes and Pharisees became more and more agitated, his words had struck a chord. Finally they yelled, "Enough!" They grabbed Stephen, those not holding him covered their ears so they could no longer hear his words. But I heard him say, "Behold, I see the heavens opened and the Son of Man standing at the right hand of God." I looked up and saw for myself the Glory of God. I basked in its warmth as the crowd began to stone Stephen. All the while this man Saul watched, with the outer cloaks of the others stashed at his feet, all the time nodding in agreement with their actions.

As Stephen died we returned to Hell. "Did you see the young man who collected the cloaks? We've seen him before. What do you recall?"

"As you know it has been my job to watch. He is from Tarsus. He is a devout Jew of the Pharisaic tradition. I have watched him since he was about 14 when he first sat at the feet of Gamaliel"

"Excellent!" Cried Satan. "He will be my instrument to destroy this Church. First in Judah, then in Samaria, and if necessary the whole world."

Lightning Source UK Ltd.
Milton Keynes UK
UKHW021217091120
373077UK00005B/804